Tess's
Saving Grace

55 Memories

Marie Woolf

United Writers Press
Asheville, N.C.

ISBN-13: 978-1-945338-30-4

Published by:

United Writers Press
Asheville, N.C.
www.unitedwriterspress.com

To contact the author, email her at:
mariewoolf@speakers-toolbox.com

Cover design by Amy Tedder
www.atyourdesign.com

First Edition

Printed in the U.S.A.

To my husband Brian, our daughter Fiona,
and my sister Kathy
who inspired, encouraged, and enriched every memory.
Love you more...

Special thanks to Vally Sharpe,
my wise and patient mentor and editor

Tess's Saving Grace

55 Memories

Prologue

Grace

And Baby Makes Two

$\mathcal{S}$he probably should never have had a child. But funny enough, I was not a mistake. In fact, I was as meticulously planned as a kidnapping with a ten-million-dollar ransom.

My mom studied the musical gene pool and then interviewed the sperm (which she called dating). She then made the unprotected move on the unsuspecting donor and gave birth without identifying the clueless father. And there I was: six pounds, six ounces of perfection that she loved, indulged, and devoted herself to for the next fifteen years.

Who was the father? The supermarket tabloids and entertainment shows went wild with speculation and insinuation. She did seem to lead a lewd and lascivious life. She was, after all, a mega famous rock star known worldwide by her first name only…Tess.

To describe her as stunning would not do her justice. She always was, and still is, to-die-for "Helen of Troy" beautiful. Thick, cobalt black hair frames her perfectly symmetrical face with its flawless white skin and velvety eyelashes. Her petite body is perfectly proportioned except for her real boobs. They seem big for her slender frame.

And then there is her musical talent. She is a singer and songwriter and plays the piano by ear. She has a powerful, sultry, sexy, soulful voice that conveys heartache yet strength, vulnerability yet confidence.

My mom is not only the leader in rock music but she is the best-selling female recording artist of all time. She has won every award for which she has been nominated including Grammys for Best New Artist, Album of the Year, Record of the Year and Song of the Year, just to name a few. No one has any doubt that she will one day be inducted into the Rock & Roll Hall of Fame.

She continues to release back–to-back hits and triple platinum albums and sells out stadiums and arenas worldwide. She has sung the National Anthem at the Super Bowl. The only thing she hasn't done is a Christmas album and I don't think she ever will.

And if that isn't enough, she is one of those people that everyone wants to be around. If there's a party and she can't come, the date is changed. If there's a dinner, everyone wants to sit next to her. If she goes out anywhere, she is photographed and mobbed by fans.

So who is my father? I don't know. There were, and still are, many men in my Mom's life and they all are crazy about her. She *is* a discriminating and selective one-man woman. She just happens to have a very short attention span. Her philosophy is that her heart can't be claimed because it's hers to give away and so far she is just not ready to do that.

Of all the men in my Mom's life, I've especially loved her fellow musicians. But my favorite is Gus, her road manager and duet partner, especially after she has had a few drinks. I used to pray that he was my father.

Handsome, honest, trustworthy, and probably an Eagle Scout in another life, he has taken care of things just like I imagine a father would — except that he gets paid for it. I bet some days no amount of money is enough for putting up with us but he is always there. Gus is our go-to guy.

I think that I am a lot like Gus. Maybe further evidence that he is my Dad? We make a good team.

I am Grace. I think Gus and I are "Tess's Saving Grace." Without us, Mom would not have been rescued or saved from herself. So I think of us as a family...in a very modern sort of way.

2

I Was Homeschooled

Growing up with Mom was...different. I was homeschooled, or at least that's what she called it. It was more like schooled on the road and schooled in the sky.

There was never a little house with a white picket fence and a "Mom and Dad." Mom never made chocolate chip cookies and we didn't have cookouts in the backyard. In fact, I've never seen her turn on the stove.

Instead, there was a limo, a tour bus, a private jet, presidential suites, and a penthouse condo in the hotel that we called home. For the longest time, I thought all food was ordered by phone and delivered on rolling carts with silver trays and fresh roses.

Mom's idea of homeschooling was not following a faith-based Christian curriculum. It was more like a real-life immersion where anything goes. Her definition of speaking with a filter meant whispering or blocking my ears with her hands. I wanted to say, "Hello! I am here in the same room and I can hear you because I haven't had rock music blaring at me for years." Unfortunately, some degree of hearing loss is an occupational hazard.

It was a rock-star life of extravagance. I was raised by a rowdy, rich, talented, creative band of musical geniuses. There was an abundance of hundred-dollar tips for coffee, thousand-dollar bottles of champagne, and million-dollar musical instruments. Life was lived with reckless abandon and I was the center of attention.

Mom and my eclectic "family" gave me everything they never had and seemed to enjoy it just as much as I did.

"Gracie needs a black leather Harley outfit and a baby Harley motorcycle with training wheels!" Done! It didn't matter that I was only two at the time.

"Wouldn't it be cool to buy Gracie a snow leopard with a diamond collar?" Done! Most five-year-olds had a rescue cat.

"Let's celebrate Gracie's half birthday!" Done! Apparently, they needed yet another excuse to celebrate.

My real birthday was in May so every November on my "half birthday," we vacationed at a different Disney resort. We went to California, Florida, Japan, France, and Hong Kong — and then we just started all over again.

My mom and her loyal band, the Boys, all lived vicariously through me. Each and every one of them came from broken homes with dysfunctional families and I was their little girl. Turns out, I became the mom to this band of misfits...and they became my family.

3

Religion vs. Rock 'n' Roll

*S*o how did I get here? By here, I mean a prestigious New England Christian boarding school in the middle of nowhere with no locks on the doors.

Is it possible to crave discipline and long for structure, monotony, and even boredom? To know that on Monday, I will wake up and do the same thing that I did last Monday.

Having never attended school, church, or AA meetings—which some of Mom's Roadies attended religiously—I had never done anything every day, at a certain time, for a certain purpose. That would not be a rock 'n' roll lifestyle.

Gus and another "family member" Teddy—tried—but late nights, wild parties, record releases, and live concerts in every part of the world, tended to get in the way.

I desperately wanted to meet people my own age. So I thought maybe I should go to school where I could lead a more "normal" life.

Where was I academically? Turns out, Mom believed in education and always managed to hire stellar tutors who instilled in me a love of learning and, most of all, reading. She went ballistic, not surprisingly, when I first advanced my plan for becoming a "schoolgirl" and attending an actual boarding school.

Picture Elizabeth Kubler-Ross's "Five Stages of Grief" — only a million times worse.

1. DENIAL: *"You won't leave us. Structure is overrated."*
2. ANGER: *"You are a minor and you are not going anywhere!"*
3. BARGAINING: *"I will buy you a Range Rover."*
4. DEPRESSION: *"What did I do? Why do you want to leave me?"*
5. ACCEPTANCE: *"I want to speak to you every day and I expect you to be with us on weekends."*

Mom reluctantly accepted my decision to start school but was never happy about it.

I quickly learned to be careful what you wish for. For the first time in my life, I was surrounded by people my own age who intimidated me. They were smart but immature, well-traveled but not worldly, liberal but not always kind.

And so, at age fifteen, I began my journey and left for boarding school. It was far more difficult than I had ever anticipated, and there were many times I wished I had never left.

Part 1

Tess

4
Parting is Not Sweet Sorrow

Tess was sixteen when she left home and started her life. She had been unwelcome, unwanted, and unloved. "Young'un, don't you bother me 'less your hairs on fire or I swear I'm gonna hurt you!" her mother told her regularly.

Tess had a twin. Her brother, Mason, died when they were born, hence her first name was Teresa and her middle name was Mason. Her mother did not deliver the anticipated son and so resented her daughter. When her mother learned that she was unable to have more children, she blamed Tess. And so, Tess spent her youth trying to appease her mother and make her proud — but never succeeded. Everything she did was compared to what her brother would have done if he had been the one to survive.

Tess was ignored, neglected, and verbally abused because whatever she did was never good enough. Until she was able to take care of herself, her clothes were often dirty and her hair unwashed. Although she tried to be invisible, she was known as the kid whose parents were always getting drunk and making fools of themselves. Essentially, Tess was emotionally abandoned by her mother. Her no-account father, who was afraid to stand up to her mother, acquiesced.

Tess did well in school but was lonely and never fit in. Her love of music was what kept her going. She spent hours every day at their old, black, scratched, and scarred upright piano; playing by ear, singing, and composing music. She had never taken a lesson. Hers was an innate ability, a natural talent.

When she played, Tess never heard a whisper of praise from her parents. Instead, she was told to "stop that racket" because her Mama and Daddy wanted to watch their shows on the television.

The day after her 16th birthday, which was not acknowledged in any way, she decided to leave home and make her way in the music industry. When she told her parents that she was leaving, they looked up from the newspaper that they had "borrowed" from their neighbor's doorstep. Sitting in their matching stained, harvest-gold recliners they shrugged and said, "OK."

Tess left her small town in South Carolina and went to... Nashville. She was no more into country music than Mozart, but she had saved only enough money from her job at the Piggly Wiggly grocery store for a bus ticket to Tennessee.

And so, Tess began her journey into the music world. It was far more difficult than she had ever imagined, but there was never a time that she wished she hadn't left.

5

The Greyhound Bus

*T*ess arrived at the station, hot and sticky, forty-five minutes before the bus's scheduled departure. She didn't know how long it would take to walk to the Greyhound station. She had never been anywhere in an air-conditioned bus before. She had never been on a train or in a plane. She had never left the state. Even though South Carolina was on the Atlantic coast, she had never seen the ocean.

SSSSWISH ... SLAM ... SSWOOP ... SEALED! The door was shut and there was no turning back now. Tess huddled against the window and clutched her backpack in front of her as she quickly rocked back and forth trying to soothe herself.

She arrived on the outskirts of Nashville at 11:00 p.m. As she disembarked, she saw her reflection in the black glass of the bus station's window and thought, "Who is that frightened girl?" She walked to a black plastic chair that was connected to about 10 others and sat down. "Now what?"

People were everywhere, and then there was no one, anywhere. The bus station was deserted. Everyone had a place to go and left... except for this one creepy-looking man. He approached her and she could smell the stench of brown liquor and tobacco from ten feet away. She knew it well. He sat down beside her and placed his arm around the back of her chair. He called her darlin' and asked if she needed a place to stay. Said he knew people who could set her up with a job dancin' for a lot of money.

Tess knew exactly what he was talking about. She'd seen plenty of those billboards on the interstate advertising "gentlemen's clubs." Although her parents were "do as I say, not as I do Christians," they did insist she attend church regularly — especially on Wednesday nights when they offered a free covered-dish supper. She had "right from wrong" beaten into her head by many a preacher and she knew dancin' half *nekked* around a pole and shakin' it for dollar bills just wasn't right.

"I told you to stay away from here!" a stern voice behind them said. As Tess turned, she saw a small African American woman with her arthritic finger pointed at Mr. Creepy. "You get your no good sorry self out that door or I'll call the po-lice."

"Shut up old lady!" he said as his upper lip curled with disdain. "We're just talkin'."

"Out!" she screamed. He got up and slowly sauntered out the door, cussing all the while under his breath.

She looked down at Tess and asked, "What happened, child, where are you going?"

Tess began sobbing uncontrollably as her new reality sunk in. She felt two small but strong arms wrap themselves around her and hold her tightly. For the first time in her life, she felt something she had never felt before ... love. She cried until she almost fell asleep.

She heard the woman softly say, "My name is Doris and this here is my husband, Ruben, and we work this night shift. We're locking up now and you can't stay here ... so I reckon you'll be coming home with us tonight."

6
Doris and Ruben

*T*ess wasn't the first child saved by Doris and Ruben. They had seen many a lost soul arrive at the bus station and shiftless scoundrels and pimps be all over them like white on rice.

This huge-hearted, childless couple never gave up on anyone. They had an abundance of love to give and shared what little material possessions they had with anyone who needed them.

Descendants of enslaved Africans, who first set foot in America at Gadsden Wharf in Charleston, South Carolina, they came from a long line of people who worked hard and loved the Lord.

That night they settled Tess in a twin bed with a homemade quilt. She felt safe and as she fell asleep, she prayed they would like her.

Her prayer was answered.

Shortly after her arrival at Doris and Ruben's, Tess tried to call her parents to tell them where she was but couldn't reach them. She thought maybe the phone had been disconnected. It wouldn't be the first time that the utilities were "suspended" because of lack of payment.

Tess was not ready to accept the possibility that they just couldn't be bothered. She still attempted to win their love even though deep down she knew she was unlovable.

The phone was not answered because days after Tess left, her parents burned to death in a catastrophic car crash. The gas tank, ruptured during the wreck, had exploded into a massive fireball that engulfed the entire vehicle. Alcohol was a major factor. Her parents considered themselves "social drinkers" — who just happened to be *very* social.

But no one had been able to let her know. They didn't know where she was. It was a week later, after repeated attempts to call her mother and father, that Tess finally spoke to a neighbor and learned of their demise.

Miss Lottie said that the landlord had already sold everything including the black upright piano that Tess loved, and which had given her the only happiness she had ever known. The rent had been past due, she said. Her last words to Tess were, "You're better off without them, child."

Tess never cried after she heard the news. She showed no emotion and expressed no feelings. She just felt alone and empty. It broke Doris's heart.

Ruben and Doris never felt so needed by someone who deemed herself so unwanted. It became their mission to save this child and show her the love that she deserved. Doris desperately wanted Tess to return to school but feared that Child Services would intervene and Tess would be relegated to the foster care system. She knew that would kill Tess as broken and fragile as she was.

So instead, Doris and Ruben helped her continue her *music* education. Their elderly friend and neighbor was a piano and voice teacher and also played the organ at their church. Once she saw how talented and eager Tess was, she happily took her on as a student as long as Tess agreed to help her around the house.

Tess had never had any formal music lessons and loved every minute of it. She had always been able to reproduce music she had heard—playing by ear—but she became fascinated by sheet music and her learning curve was exponential.

Tess was "discovered" at, of all places, Grace Baptist Church on Viola Street. During the time she stayed with Ruben and Doris, Tess attended church regularly and sang the hymns she knew and loved. She was the only white face amongst the loving and welcoming congregation. One day, she was asked to sing *Amazing Grace* at a funeral for an old friend of Ruben's. Also attending the service was the homegrown Reverend Johnnie Johnson, the famous preacher and connoisseur of music and lovely ladies.

Reverend Johnson "knew people who knew people." He introduced Tess to a very popular and successful televangelist who preached every Sunday and appealed for funds the other six days of the week. He welcomed Tess, a beautiful and talented young girl, with open arms.

Tess's relationship with gospel only lasted about six months. At age seventeen and a half she met Jack, the man who would become her new manager. Jack recognized Tess's natural ability the minute he saw her on the Gospel station one night as he was flipping through the channels. It took a hefty cash donation for the evangelical preacher to part with Tess but he was willing to do it for the "cause."

Tess crossed over, some say to the dark side, from gospel to rock and all of the baggage that comes with a life lived on the road.

As abruptly as that chapter of her life ended, the next one began. It seemed like one day she became an orphan and the next day she was a star. She went from a teenager nobody wanted to someone everyone wanted a part of.

Tess started performing in small venues and opening for other bands all around the country. She kept in touch with Doris and Ruben by writing letters. They "weren't much for talkin' on the phone" so she wrote about her new life in letters that Doris kept and tied with a pink ribbon, and postcards that she proudly displayed on her white refrigerator.

In less than a year with Jack, Tess saved enough money to buy Doris and Ruben a brand-new silver Chevrolet. The preacher at their church had one that they often admired.

"That is one fine automobile," Doris would say to Ruben. And as it was his style to always agree with her, Ruben would say, "Yes, Doris, it's one fine automobile."

It was delivered to their driveway with a big red bow on it and a tag that read: "Thank you. I love you, Tess." It was the first time in her life that she had ever written those words to anyone — much less said them.

7

Sex, Drugs, and Rock 'n' Roll

Jack, Tess's new manager, put together a backup-band that Tess nicknamed "the Boys" (Kyle on keyboard, Petie on guitar, and JoJo on the drums) and they began touring. When Tess and the Boys started performing rock 'n' roll on the road, their innocence was quickly lost. Once lost, it can never be found again.

Tess experimented and made many, many, many poor decisions concerning alcohol, drugs and sex; one year of debauchery became two…and then three.

17 years old…Blur-r-r-r-r-r-r-r-r
18 years old…Blur-r-r-r-r-r-r-r-r
19 years old…Blur-r-r-r-r-r-r-r-r

Tess and the Boys were living large and becoming very successful. They were performing all over the United States and Canada. The first time they heard themselves on the radio was a banner day they would never forget. They celebrated by drinking way too many Hop, Skip and Go Nakeds. Life was good.

And then one day, Jack asked Tess to sign something. She had suspected for some time that Jack did not have her best interest at heart. There were several things he had done that didn't seem quite right, but she had just let it slide. For the first time—and to his chagrin—she asked, "What is this?"

He was tripling his salary. Wham! She was literally whacked upside the head.

Tess realized that she could not trust Jack anymore. Despondent because of the unscrupulous treatment she had received, she reached deep into her past and tried to become as uncaring, distant, and manipulative as her parents had been.

She vowed no one would hurt or take advantage of her again. No one was going to get close to her and no one was going to make a fool out of her. *Fool me once, shame on you; fool me twice, shame on me.*

That was her intention, anyway. Turns out all of that bravado was a façade. She was as good an actor as she was a musician. One thing for certain was that as Tess was about to enter her twenties, she really did feel lost and alone and desperately wanted to gain control of her life.

Come to find out, *When the pupil is ready, the teacher appears.*

8

Guardian Angel Gus

*R*uben had written that his old friend, John, from the Vietnam War, had come to visit them. Ruben had saved his life and every year on May 10th, the day Ruben dragged him to safety, John drove from North Carolina with a basket full of food and a honey-baked ham.

After the visit, Ruben wrote to Tess: "Doris fixed her potlikker soup, hoppin' john, collards and cornbread, even though it wasn't even New Year's Day. Everyone done cleaned their plates. She is really something." Ruben adored Doris and she adored him right back.

Since Ruben and Doris had retired, the colorful stories from the bus station had evolved into what they had for supper and what each doctor's visit entailed. It didn't matter. Tess read every letter again and again. She kept them in a messenger bag and wherever she went, they went with her.

Because of health issues, Ruben's friend, John, could no longer drive. Since his wife had passed in early March, his 24-year-old grandson Gus, a "college boy" who graduated with an international business degree, drove him to Tennessee.

Gus was working in the music industry. He loved music and was performing in any venue that would have him, hoping to make a name for himself.

Ruben had never asked for anything of Tess until that letter. "Might you know of anyone who could give him a chance?"

Of course she did! Tess would do anything for Ruben and Miss Doris.

She thought she heard Ruben say he was a rapper. Tess tried to picture a rapper "college boy" with an international business degree. There were just too many oxymorons in that salad of a sentence.

An appointment was arranged for Tess and Gus to meet. Of course, Tess was late, despite trying to be on time. At that point in her life, she thought that what she was doing was far more important than what anyone else was doing. She was always late, which was theoretically impossible because at *some* time, she'd have to mess up and be *on* time.

Tess walked in, hung-over and disheveled, but determined to help the only people who had ever loved her.

Turns out Gus was a talented musician — albeit not a talented rapper — by the name of John Augustus McCall IV.

9

A Man Of Few Words

*A*nd he was a Southern gentleman. He had this square-chiseled jaw that reminded Tess of the heroes she had seen in comic books. He stood when she walked in the room and smiled at her with big white teeth. He nodded when she spoke like he understood and respected what she said. She had never met anyone like him and felt dizzy as she tried to control the dialogue.

Tess had never interviewed or hired anyone before. Her manager, Jack, had taken care of everything. Tess's half of the exchange was strained and forced to say the least — not exactly scintillating repartee.

"So, you sing?"

Gus nodded. "Yes, I do."

"Play anything?"

"The saxophone."

"So what's your sign?" *Dang, did I just say that out loud,* she thought.

"Umm...Capricorn."

After a few more moments of stilted conversation she finally said, "OK, you're hired." Neither one of them knew what he was going to do, but both knew it felt right.

When Jack found out, he was livid. "How dare she do that!" he thought. He knew he had to be careful, though, because Tess was, after all, the money machine. Tess and the Boys had been handpicked by Jack and he would have to find some way to get rid of this intruder.

Gus was introduced to everyone and had no trouble fitting in, even though he was different. Unlike Tess and the Boys, his family life had been "normal." His parents weren't abusive alcoholics like Tess's, low-life gamblers like Kyle's dad, promiscuous junkies like Petie's mom, or shiftless losers like the woman who gave birth to JoJo.

Gus and his parents were educated, church-going, valuable members of their community. He'd grown up with wealth and the privileges that came with it.

He spent his summers sailing at the beach and waterskiing at the lake. In the fall, he excelled at tennis and, on weekends, he tailgated at his parents alma mater which later became his as well.

Winter was busy with snowskiing in the mountains. In the spring, he played golf and impressed everyone at the Country Club—especially his proud Dad, because his golf game just got better and better.

And then, of course, there was the family "va-ca" as he loved to call the annual family vacation. His favorite vacation memory was not a motel pool. Instead, he and his family traveled the world. By the time Gus was twenty-one, he had visited all seven continents and had lost count of the number of countries.

But he didn't let his upbringing get in the way of befriending Tess and the Boys. Gus listened to their tawdry stories, put up with their foul language and, in very short order, steered the band further into stardom. Why? They all knew why. Tess.

The only person Gus did not win over was Jack. Tess knew Jack was living large because of her, but so was everyone else. She didn't begin to know how to find someone else to replace him and so she accepted his authority as he manipulated her in his own obsequious way.

Like a guardian angel, Gus quietly began to point out inconsistencies and discrepancies in management, fairness, and, especially, payroll. Tess and the Boys had no idea how successful they were or what they were worth. They were happy because they loved what they were doing. It was their passion and they shared that passion with their audiences, fans, and all the groupies that appeared after their concerts.

Gus discovered that Jack was investing a ton of Tess's money, but not on her behalf. Tess was signing documents and Jack was buying houses, cars, and boats for himself. Trouble was no one else owned anything, not even a bank account, except Jack.

"That boy needs to mind his own business," Jack said to Tess. "We are kin and he is about on my last nerve."

10

Come to Jesus Meeting

Gus had drunk the Kool-Aid and was all in. These people were beginning to feel like family, albeit relatives he was glad not to be sharing the same gene pool with.

Gus felt it was time to come clean with what he had learned about Jack—but how? In Tess's and the Boys' minds, all was going well. They were living in the present, minute to minute, and enjoying life in the fast lane.

For someone like Gus, without a job description or title, it would be easy for his role to just disappear. So, after a long talk with his dad, an entertainment lawyer, he decided it was time.

He began with Tess, telling her how much money was coming in. He laid it all out like a business model. "I'm just rolled over and tickled! Dang, I'm rich!" Tess exclaimed.

"Yes, but where is it? You really need to think about a 401(k)... blah, blah, blah."

Or at least that's what it sounded like to Tess.

Gus then tried another approach. JoJo, her drummer, and Petie, her lead guitarist, were always talking about wanting kids. "Don't you want to have money to pay for your kid's college education?" he asked.

"Blah, blah, blah," they heard. No one had gone to college and would have a hard time saving for something that wasn't necessary in their minds.

And then Gus remembered Natalie. She was "Keyboard Kyle's" only child. Tess occasionally slipped into her Southern roots with all of its colloquialisms and would often lament, "Bless her heart, she ain't right. No baby should have that many broken bones." Kyle wanted to make sure Natalie, his sweet little girl, was always taken care of and so finally Gus's words did not fall on deaf ears.

That became the back door that Gus came through when he exposed Jack. Sure, Jack had been "takin' care of business" yesterday and today, but maybe someday, sometime, they needed to start thinking about tomorrow.

Jack had been robbing them blind but, in his mind, there was still enough to go around—just not equally. He was furious when Gus and Tess confronted him. Tess demanded to see key documents, tax returns, and the contract she signed as a minor. Jack, caught unawares, did not have time to "doctor" or shred the evidence.

Gus had done his due diligence. Jack knew he was busted, but the unctuous bastard still attempted to claim the rights to some songs. Gus threatened a lawsuit and Jack had no choice but to acquiesce.

When all was said and done, Tess wanted comeuppance. She wanted to trash-talk Jack and slap him into tomorrow. Gus convinced her that the only person who would suffer would be her. Tess needed to let it go, Gus said. That's how you make peace. Trust that justice would prevail.

And it did, in Tess's mind. Once asked by the press why Jack was no longer her manager, she replied, "He lied, cheated, and stole millions from me." Although Jack was a very wealthy man, he was ostracized and treated as a pariah by those in the industry—to Jack, a fate worse than death. To Tess, it was justice—poetic justice.

Gus became the man. He was the business manager, mediator, money-man and go-to guy who morphed into a daddy-like figure that everyone could rely on. The doctor was always in. No one depended on him more than Tess even though she was loathe to admit it.

11
What's a Weekend?

Gus had inherited a handful. He soon learned many more of the reasons why the band was so successful.

Despite being a manipulative crook, Jack had an incredible eye and ear for talent. And once found, he would coil around it like kudzu on a sapling.

Finding Tess had been a coup. She was an extraordinarily talented singer and after she became his new client, Jack was astounded to discover the incredible repertoire of songs that Tess had already written. They were *really* good and he knew they would be hits.

Jack then found the band. He knew exactly what he wanted. They couldn't be too smart. In terms of intellect, Jack wanted them to realize that education was not for everyone. He wanted minds that were not fully developed in terms of their frontal lobes. They didn't need to make good decisions. That was his job. No one over age 25 need apply. Jack had a plan.

They had to be young, really good-looking males with no families to speak of. They had to be able to compose music, play at least two instruments, and sing really well. During the audition, they had to perform songs they had written. He wanted raw talent that would take off running. Jack was in a hurry.

On top of all that, everyone had to get along. There would be no alpha male, just good ol' Southern boys doing what they loved. Jack knew they would be as strong as their weakest link, so he made sure there was no weak link.

The band would have no name. Tess was the star and they were the back-up musicians. The group couldn't take a bad picture, especially with Tess in their midst. She was beautiful and everybody knew it...except her.

Even though they could have been successful performing in many genres, Jack insisted on rock 'n' roll. They were going to become the Bad Boys of Rock, even if their actions never matched the trash they read about themselves in the tabloids.

The Boys were far from saints, and Jack used that fact to generate scandalous publicity quickly, even if it wasn't true. If they received attention for bad behavior, it was not only better than no attention at all, he thought—it was to be celebrated! He knew which photographers to call to snap the required lewd photos when things got out of hand. Jack was despicable but he was making them famous and they let him.

But Jack was careful as he crafted their "bad boy" image. He knew Tess and the Boys liked to have a good time, but he certainly didn't want to sabotage their careers or his bulging paycheck. So, when groupies, hangers-on, and wannabes came back to the hotel with them, he had them patted down and made them sign waivers and non-disclosure agreements. Jack was a cautious man.

They all worked hard, played hard, and lived every day like it was their last and every night like it was their first.

Groupies came and groupies went but *they* were meant to be together forever. Who says arranged marriages don't work?

There was never any need to wait for a weekend to have fun. Every day was a weekend.

12

The Star and Gus

*I*t's complicated...

Tess thrived under Gus's tutelage. Although she had endured hardships as a child, she was a survivor by nature and necessity.

She was a keen songwriter and Gus encouraged her to dig deep into her colorful redneck roots of confusion and pain. To Gus, she came from a long line of raconteurs. To Tess, she was spawned by "lyin' scum."

Writing was cathartic for Tess. As a child, she was never allowed to express her feelings so there was a lot of pent-up anger, isolation, and sadness that in the past she would eschew, but not now. It all came out and, though the lyrics were current and relatable, the feelings were timeless. Her new songs were poignant yet still full of hope—something Jack would never have allowed.

Music was Tess's drug of choice. She appeared laid back but her energy and emotions would rise to a crescendo of misery unless she could compose, play, and sing. And she was driven. She didn't exactly have a temper but she could be short with people if a piano wasn't available for her to pound on.

During the first three years under Gus's guidance, money *really* started rolling in. There was so much it was as if they were printing it. Gus was carefully investing for everyone but they were also enjoying a very extravagant lifestyle. Life was good...and then it got better.

Tess finally released her first full-length album and was nominated for the Best New Artist Grammy Award. The awards ceremony was surreal for them as they sat amongst their idols.

When Tess's name was announced as the winner, she looked at Gus, the Boys, and Doris and Ruben and said, "Thank you. Love you." She knew she didn't do this on her own. It took a family and they were her family.

Gus loved what he was doing. It was not the career in international business that his father had imagined for him, but it was a business that he was running. He jumped in headfirst and learned fast. There were no classes you could take on how to cope with a band full of free-spirited mischievous musicians who had no desire to grow up. But he persevered and soon was juggling all of the "goof balls" in the air at the same time.

"Man, you work too hard," Gus was told over and over again. The Boys were so glad they weren't "college boys" because all they had to do was play music and not deal with paperwork and problems.

Gus knew everyone thought he was a workaholic but, hey, the money was great, he was getting to see the world, and he was singing and playing his sax more and more with the band.

And then, of course, there was Tess. He would never admit that he was over-the-moon stupid in love with her. But he was. He had fallen for this wounded, fragile, vulnerable woman, and Tess had submitted to this honest, caring, and faithful man...to a point.

If happiness is defined as having love, laughter, friendship and purpose in your life, then they had it all. It was an unfamiliar state for Tess but she really, really liked it. So much so that she wanted to share it.

So...Tess decided to have a baby.

Oh, and By the Way...

Apart from Doris, there were no women in Tess's life. She had no girlfriends, relatives, or even acquaintances that she could call. The revolving door of women the Boys brought in were not exactly the maternal types.

So, when she confirmed that she was indeed "with child," Tess paid a visit to Doris and Ruben to share the good news before it exploded in the tabloids.

"You are just glowing, child," cooed Doris. "Tell me all about your plans."

There really were no plans beyond that point. Tess thought she would have the baby and she would be a good mother and she would love this baby with all her heart. And Doris knew she would.

Doris also knew she had no idea what she was getting herself into — especially because she wanted to raise this child and not share the identity of the father. Tess told Doris, "It's not as if I don't want to get married at some point. I just don't want to get divorced."

Doris knew otherwise. Tess was afraid to open her heart and let anyone in. Doris and Ruben loved Tess more than any other child they had rescued but it had taken Tess more time to reciprocate that love. It was hard for her to give love when she had never known it. She thought she was unlovable because it was easier to believe the bad stuff she had heard about herself all of her life. Eventually, Tess learned for herself that Doris and

Ruben's love was selfless and unconditional and that they would never abandon her.

Still, Doris worried about Tess. Ruben would assure her by saying, "Doris don't you fret, none. That li'l girl will figure it out."

Like everything in Tess's world, it would evolve.

Very early on in her pregnancy, on the way home from Europe after a very successful tour, Tess told the Boys about the baby. They had stayed up late telling stories and drinking bottles of Cristal. Except for Tess—she drank Perrier.

Tess entertained them with a story from her youth. "One of Daddy's drinking buddies once fished a valise out of Low Rock Lake with a human head in it. He was interviewed by reporters, of course, and the next day the newspaper's headline was *Head Found in Valise, Foul Play Suspected.*" The Boys about fell on the floor laughing.

After a few more stories, Tess stood up. "I'm going to call it a night and rest for a few hours." She walked away and then stopped, turning back to face them. "Oh, and by the way, I'm pregnant."

Petie looked at JoJo. "Did she say regnant? What does regnant mean?"

JoJo seemed just as confused. "No, I think she said fragrant."

Wide-eyed, Kyle whispered, "No, guys, she said PREGNANT!"

"Oh-h-h-h-h-h-h," they all whispered as the reality sunk in. No one knew what to think or say.

Later, as they attempted to rest, each of the Boys began to remember snippets of their own childhoods and the emotional baggage they had to bear. Kyle had aged out of the foster care system after being in numerous homes. As a little boy, there were many families who wanted to adopt him but his father wouldn't give up his parental rights. He hoped he would get himself together and get his son back but booze and gambling always got in the way. On rare occasions, he would visit Kyle, drunk and on his liquor-cycle. And then he just stopped coming.

Petie was born to a single mother with a drug addiction problem she couldn't beat. They lived on government assistance and at an early age, he became the parent to the parent he loved. He never had a childhood. Petie was seventeen when his mother collapsed for the last time and died on a familiar street corner. She was thirty-three.

JoJo's single mother depended on her kind and loving elderly neighbors in the trailer park to help her care for her infant son. One day, she left for the weekend with her new boyfriend and never returned. Everyone thought they were JoJo's grandparents anyway so they raised him as their own.

The Boys loved Tess but didn't know what to do or what to expect. They were not deep thinkers so didn't try to figure out what this would mean for them in the future. Tess seemed happy so they decided to be happy, too, and see what happened next.

Tess had a textbook pregnancy and decided to deliver the baby at a private hospital in South Carolina. The hospital staff had never seen such a colorful crew of men. Everybody wondered which one of them was going to be the new daddy, given they all seemed so interested in Tess's contractions, dilations, and overall health.

A nurse came into the room where the Boys were waiting. "It won't be too long now."

"How many seconds between contractions?" asked Kyle, biting his fingernail.

Petie jumped up. "Has she asked for an epidural?"

"Can you tell if it's a boy or a girl yet?" asked JoJo.

Everyone was interested in her birth canal.

"I can't believe people do this every day!" shouted Tess. Her goal was to deliver the baby naturally and she succeeded, because by the time she screamed, "Epidural!" it was too late. Baby Grace arrived full term with long piano fingers and the cry of a soprano. Gus and the Boys all wiped back tears of relief and happiness.

They took turns holding Grace and made a contest out of what they were going to teach her, give her, and where they would take her:

"I want her to see China. Remember how much fun we had there?" said Petie.

"I'm going to take her to Antarctica. She can play with the penguins," JoJo said as he imitated their waddle.

"How about the moon!" Kyle exclaimed. And he was supposed to be the smart one.

Tess fell asleep that night knowing Baby Grace had a family with lots of daddies and a mama who loved her.

The good news was that Tess did not want a nanny. Or was that the bad news? Either way, she was going to be a hands-on mother.

In reality, Tess was deathly afraid of failing at motherhood. She didn't want anyone watching her make mistakes. In order for Grace to feel loved, Tess decided that she would have to do exactly the opposite of what her mama and daddy did. Tess would tell Grace every day that she loved her. She would never say, "No," to her and she would give her anything she wanted. Well, that was the plan, anyway.

Although no one had ever seen her read a book, when Tess became pregnant, she became a voracious reader of baby books. She had never babysat but she had good instincts and a commonsense approach. Even with this knowledge, it was still touch and go.

In the hospital, Tess was exhausted but stubborn. "I can do this," she insisted, even though she looked like a child cradling a baby doll. Every time the baby cried, she would rock her to sleep with her favorite hymns, especially *Amazing Grace*. When Tess held her, she was in awe of this little miracle. She thought of her own childhood and quietly wept as she wondered, "Why couldn't you love me, Mama?"

The day Tess left the hospital with Grace was a nightmare. The paparazzi had always stalked Tess but with the imminent arrival of the baby, the press grew exponentially and was far more aggressive. Gus always hired top-notch security that was everpresent but unobtrusive. Still, Tess felt claustrophobic and never developed a relationship with any of the bodyguards.

She had always shunned the idea of a personal bodyguard for herself. The security team protected all of them from the fans and the press. She mostly traveled in a pack with the Boys anyway and they hardly ever went out during the day. They all had serious Vitamin-D deficiencies.

The delivery hospital was supposed to be kept secret but someone had tipped off the media. Every exit was teeming with reporters and photographers trying to capture the first picture.

A doctor wheeled Tess and the baby out in the required wheelchair and all hell broke loose. Security surrounded her as she attempted to enter the car. Pushing, shoving and shouting came from everywhere.

"Tess, Tess, who's the Baby Daddy?"

"Was it a mistake?

"Is it a boy or girl?"

Tess had always given the press a chance to take photos when she was out even though she feigned disgust. But this was different. She felt like she was being intentionally harassed.

With her hormones raging and fear escalating, she clutched Grace and stepped into the back of the car. As Gus jumped into the front, she told the driver to floor it. The press did not get their shot and wanted her charged with child endangerment, as Grace was not put in a car seat until they could stop safely and out of range of the media onslaught.

"We don't need a nanny, but we sure as hell need a full-time personal bodyguard for the baby!" she said in an audibly shaking voice. "We have to protect her."

Gus immediately started interviewing candidates. He wanted someone who could understand the lifestyle. Tess wanted someone who would fit in.

Finally, Gus had six near-perfect candidates. Tess and the Boys sat in during the interviews and later discussed each applicant. Unreasonable and ridiculous could not even begin to describe some of the band's objections:

"I didn't like his shoes. I don't think I could trust him with that kind of taste."

Gus was incredulous. "Really, his shoes!"

"That is one serious dude. He has no sense of humor."

Gus, exasperated, simply replied, "He is very qualified."

"He was packin', and I don't like to *see* guns."

"Guys, guys," Gus said as patiently as he could. "Bodyguards carry guns. This is our reality."

All six applicants were deep-sixed. Gus was frustrated because he desperately wanted to get someone in place as quickly as possible.

Then Tess remembered Thaddeus Ray, Doris's great-nephew. They were always bragging on him because he was a "military man and a good boy." He was leaving the service and had been offered a position with the F.B.I., but he agreed to meet with Tess at Doris's urging.

The group gathered, this time with the baby.

"Hi everybody, I'm Teddy," he said as he nodded to everyone. "And this must be little Grace. What a beauty," he cooed as he touched her little foot. It was obvious Teddy had been around kids before. In fact, he had been around lots of them—he was the oldest of seven children. He had attended two years of community college while he worked as a police officer and then had joined the military. He had become an officer and had served two tours as an Army Ranger.

The interview began with the same questions Gus had asked the other six. This time, however, it was different. The band was in awe of this veteran and interested in his time in the war.

"Ever drive one of those armored vehicles?"

"Can you fly a helicopter?"

"I had a G.I. Joe that looked just like you!"

Tess was also in awe, interested in the man she knew would keep Grace safe. This felt right, just like she knew the first time she met Gus.

Gus was also impressed. Teddy was easy going, competent, and articulate There was actually another adult in the room to have an intelligent conversation with. Gus knew he had his head on straight when he asked if the medical plan included dental. "Sure, anything you want," Gus replied.

Tess now had two men in her life she could not only trust with her life, but more importantly, with Grace's life. Teddy was a big beautiful man and Gus was a gorgeous gentle giant. They were her ebony and ivory.

15

At Home in a Hotel

Tess would not even allow a crib to be set up in her condo until she delivered the baby and everything was OK.

Sure, the Boys bought things every day, and after oohing and aahing over them, she would put them in big plastic bins that overflowed with baby dolls, stuffed animals, and gifts that were totally not age-appropriate. "This baseball glove is awesome! Thank you so much, Jojo," said Tess.

She had no intention of putting the baby in a dresser drawer. In fact, she had designed two nurseries, one for a boy and another for a girl. As soon as she delivered, a staff of 25 professionals would totally transform a suite into the nursery—kind of like an Amish barn-raising.

Until Gus came, Tess and the Boys lived mostly in hotels and rented luxury homes and stayed put until the next gig. If they were in Los Angeles and the next show was in New York in two weeks, then they holed up in Los Angeles for two weeks. They stored stuff everywhere and when they couldn't remember where it was, they just bought it all over again. They were burning through money and earning it right back.

The hotel suites cost tens of thousands of dollars, plus room service bills. For a price, you would not believe what you could have delivered: furs and jewelry for the latest groupie; a helicopter parked on the roof for nightly "city lights" tours; and Gus's personal favorite, an orchestra. At first, he was furious, but everyone later agreed that was one of the best nights ever.

Over time, Tess and the Boys began to calm down. Then again, maybe their lifestyle just became the norm. They still loved to throw a "little party" in every city, and the cleanup and damage fees had to be dealt with, as well as the tips for the maids. In some cases, the maids were also the recipients of the furs and the jewelry. Hotels were only too happy to take their money, and hotel security was only too happy to see them leave.

Gus thought they needed a home base to come back to—not to mention more investments. He hoped "pride of ownership" might make them a little more responsible. Atlanta made the most sense as it was easy to get in and out of and offered the nightlife they craved.

The Boys said:

"Yeah, sounds OK as long as we can live in a hotel."

"Man, we need that concierge!"

"And room service!"

With this wish list in mind, Gus searched availability. A fabulous new hotel was under construction and the penthouse floor was available. They were able to customize the 20,000 square-foot space and divide it into two condos with a grand piano in each.

The Boys and Gus shared one condo with four master suites and Tess lived in the other, which had three master suites. The condos shared a private keyed elevator and a grand foyer with a huge round antique walnut table in the center. A seasonal arrangement of fresh-cut flowers from all around the world was displayed there and changed daily.

Turns out, they liked playing house in a hotel.

"So, we don't have to pack up? We can leave our stuff here?"

"Yeah, you own it man," Gus replied.

When Tess became pregnant, she wondered if they needed a house. She had torn out all kinds of glossy pictures from magazines featuring beautiful houses with luxury nurseries and custom-made swing sets in the backyard. The Boys also began collecting pictures and had all kinds of decorating ideas and tips for Tess:

"Let's build a garage and collect cars! I want a Bugatti Chiron!"

"And trucks! I want a big ol' tricked out Ford pickup!"

"And boats! We need a cigarette boat! Those babies can fly!"

Tess thought, "Boys and their toys."

Gus knew the Boys were not ready for suburbia and even questioned whether Tess was. In any case, he knew suburbia was not ready for them. The cliché, "There goes the neighborhood," would be written all over their new neighbor's faces.

They really didn't spend that much time in Atlanta and it was Tess's intention to homeschool the baby and keep her with her. So how practical was this idea of a house anyway?

The hotel security and staff at the condo were excellent, so Gus convinced Tess that the baby would be safer in the condo of a secure hotel than a home in a neighborhood. Plus, everyone loved room service and all of the amenities the hotel had to offer like the restaurant, pool and bar.

So, after Grace was born, Tess had one of the suites in her condo turned into a nursery. "Does it look like the picture? I want it to look just like this picture," she asked everyone who came through the door. In reality it looked better. It was magnificent. The beautifully appointed nursery was fit for a princess and had the intoxicating smell of a newborn baby.

Everything was white and gray with soft touches of pink. An elaborate Waterford crystal chandelier hung from the high ceiling. Voluminous pale pink silk drapes covered the windows and puddled on the floor.

Built-in white bookcases with lower cabinets flanked either side of the white fireplace and contained bunnies, bears, and baby dolls in muted colors of pink, white, and gray. Two white upholstered high-backed swivel rockers and ottomans sat on each side of the fireplace with soft pink cashmere throws casually draped over them.

The entry door was framed by huge, white carved and mirrored armoires. An extra-wide and extra-long white changing table held everything the baby would ever need.

And then there was the crib. It was exquisite—hand-carved and painted white with a pale pink silk dust ruffle and big pale pink silk bows tied at each corner.

The only thing missing was the baby. Although Grace napped in her nursery, she slept each night in her custom-made bassinet in Tess's room — just in case she needed her mama.

To accommodate Teddy, Gus moved from the Boys' condo into the empty third suite in Tess's. Teddy took Gus's place in the fourth suite in the Boys' condo.

Teddy became the bodyguard extraordinaire. Tess may not have had a nanny but she sure did have a "manny" in Teddy. He could shoot a gun, keep clamoring fans at bay, and change a diaper!

Every day, he proudly strolled Baby Grace around the hotel in her giant Silver Cross Balmoral English pram with its big white tires. The boys joked that they could take Gracie off-roading in it and she would never even feel a bump. It was one smooth ride.

Soon Teddy and Grace knew everyone in the hotel and they knew them. "Here comes little Miss Grace with Teddy!" they would exclaim. Everyone would stop what they were doing and they would all come out to see the beautiful baby in her latest designer outfit and discuss how she was growing.

Who said a hotel couldn't be a home?

16

Old Habits Die Hard

*E*veryone was young, hyper, and full of raging hormones. To say they took part in high risk and reckless activities would be an understatement. This pattern of behavior led to dangerous situations that most people would learn from and not repeat. But they were not most people.

Until Grace came along, smoking was not an issue anyone wanted to address. It didn't matter that they almost burnt down two hotels and a beach house—they craved nicotine.

Their idea of a "breakfast of champions" consisted of copious amounts of Coca-Cola and cigarettes. The chain-smoking continued throughout the day and night. At day's end and after a nightcap of Jack, there was always one long final drag on a cigarette. A blue haze of smoke assaulted anyone who walked through the front door of the Boys' penthouse.

No matter how many ashtrays Gus had on every table, the Boys excelled at missing their mark. Gus finally bought huge metal fire pits and placed them in their penthouse. The butts found their way there only because they made it a tossing competition, but the ashes were still everywhere.

When Tess became pregnant, she sat down with the Boys and shared photos and stories of babies born to mothers who had smoked, drunk alcohol, and/or used drugs. She explained that second-hand smoke was dangerous, especially to a baby's lungs.

The Boys sat in heavy silence and then finally all agreed in unison that the baby should never be allowed to smoke. Gus gasped incredulously. "Guys, this is about *you*. Just don't smoke inside the condo anymore, OK?"

"Oh, yeah. OK."

The Boys were making an effort but the going was rough. It was not until Grace arrived and Teddy was hired that Tess announced some changes needed to take place immediately concerning smoking.

Teddy was relieved and borderline euphoric. When Teddy first arrived, he thought that the Boys were witty and clever and therefore must be kidding with some of the things they said or suggested. He quickly learned, however, that despite being talented musicians, they were not, and would never be, the sharpest knives in the drawer.

The Boys' behavior was particularly at odds with Teddy because he had no relationship with alcohol, drugs, or nicotine. His body was a temple that he respected and nourished appropriately. It was also his job to make sure all the butts were out at night. It was a hard job.

Gus wrote a list of suggestions. They were never called rules because these lovable rogues knew rules were only made to be broken:

No smoking or vaping in Tess's penthouse.

Vaping allowed inside Boy's penthouse only.

Cigarette smoking allowed on balcony only.

This was a monumental challenge and they did look for loopholes:

"But bongs are OK, right?"

"Can we use lighters?"

"Where can hot girls smoke?"

Tess knew the Boys would eventually come around, but Teddy had his doubts. He did not think they could be depended upon to do anything except play music.

He was wrong. Teddy had underestimated the love and devotion they had for Tess and each other.

17

A "Fractured" Fairy Tale Life

*P*eople say a baby changes your life. For the most part and for most people that is probably true. But, remember, Tess and her merry band were not most people. They were stars and rules didn't apply to them—or so they were led to believe. Consequences were not something they had to deal with.

Gus was continually putting out fires for stupid shenanigans, skylarking, youthful hijinks, silly antics, and pranks that the Boys and Tess thought nothing of at the time.

In one week, Gus paid a fine because one of them drove the wrong way down a one-way street — in reverse. "I thought it would look like I was going in the right direction," said Kyle.

He replaced an entire floor of hotel carpeting after one of them peed in the hallway. "Man, I went through the wrong door," said Petie.

And he made a hefty donation to try and appease the animal rights activists when one of the Boys strapped an iguana on his head and went to a party with nothing else on but a flesh-colored speedo. "That iguana was into it!" said JoJo.

Tess was Peter Pan and her band—the Lost Boys—were brilliant musicians entering adulthood but who would never grow up. They lived that old adage, "Growing old may be mandatory but growing up was optional."

Gus would talk and talk and talk to them and they would nod and nod and nod right back at him. They never took correction as an assault. Instead, they would agree, "Yeah that was pretty stupid, yeah, yeah, yeah, I get it." Then Gus would leave and he would hear them giggling about how cool that iguana was and hear, "Let's get Baby Gracie one. Every little baby needs one."

Gus would make yet another mental note of prohibited items for the hotel concierge to reinforce: "No pets allowed in the penthouses. Especially iguanas."

Deep down, they were all loyal decent guys who had never known constructive discipline, except when it came to their music. When it was time to practice and perform, they were all in, heart and soul. So Gus put up with the reckless questionable behavior as long as the answer to two questions was "No." (1) Was it illegal? (2) Would anyone get hurt? Even then, allowances were made.

They would never change. It would be up to Grace to fit in and thrive in this chaos. Everyone loved having her around, buying her outfits and toys, and photographing and recording every cute thing she said and did...

When Grace was two, one of her many friends and admirers, the hotel doorman, was trying to get her to talk and asked her Teddy's name. "Who is that nice man with you?" Grace looked up at Teddy and replied, "My Teddy Bear."

She was a quiet happy child who took it all in. She grew up hearing too much, seeing too much, and learning too much of all the wrong things. Precocious, with an excellent vocabulary, she often repeated things she heard, much to the chagrin of Gus and Teddy but to the delight of Tess and the Boys. At three, she knew far too many cuss words and she used them appropriately...

One rainy morning, Grace wanted to take a walk and splash in the puddles. She put on her rain boots, Paddington Bear-yellow raincoat, and matching rain hat. Her favorite umbrella with the duck handle set the outfit off nicely she thought, as she admired herself in the mirror. But she wasn't finished yet. She opened her custom-made cabinet and from the ten designers represented, she chose Cazal. She knew the perfect accessory to every outfit— sunglasses.

Out she walked, with Teddy in tow, only to discover that the rain had stopped. She looked up at her friend, the doorman, and as she stamped her foot she said, "Damn, the rain stopped!"

The doorman had to muffle his laughter and look away. "Yes, Miss Grace, the rain has stopped," he said. And to Teddy, he apologized for laughing, "Sorry, Teddy, it won't happen again." Even though he knew Grace would never fail to amuse him.

Teddy gave the doorman a look of disapproval and gently said to Grace, "I know you can do better than that. Please try again."

"OK, Teddy Bear...Damn, the sun's out?" she half asked. Sometimes, Teddy wondered if Grace was messing with him.

Gus and Teddy were Grace's disciplinarians. They never raised their voices but, by example, they taught her how to be polite, mind her manners, and tell the truth, which sometimes backfired.

Yes ma'am, no ma'am, yes sir, and *no sir* were all part of her vocabulary. She looked people in the eye when they spoke to her and she loved shaking people's hands. She even learned how to write thank you notes. She was a Southern girl through and through.

Dear Miss Doris and Ruben,
Thank you for the red birdhouse. It is my third favorite color.
Love, Gracie
PS. I miss y'all. Come see us!

18

Sparrow

"Keyboard Kyle" had a daughter, Natalie. Although she lived with her mother, she spent a great deal of time with her daddy when he was in Atlanta. He adored her because she was adorable. There was not a mean bone in her body—trouble was, there wasn't a strong one either.

Natalie was born with *Osteogenesis Imperfecta* or Brittle Bone Disease. She came home from the hospital in a cast and pretty much stayed in one, for one reason or another, all of her life.

Natalie's nickname was Sparrow because she did remind you of a delicate little bird. She had a head full of soft brown "Shirley Temple" curls that were always in her eyes. She had tiny doll-like features with big brown eyes that twinkled. She was a kind, good-natured, gentle child with a big sweet smile.

And Grace worshipped her.

Natalie was three years older than Grace and the only childhood friend she had ever known. They were tighter than ticks. Grace loved coming home to Atlanta and being with Sparrow. Because of a "W" for "R" substitution, Grace called her "Spawwow" for the longest time.

With the Boys, Grace was all rough and tumble. They raced, raged, and roamed the world together. But with Sparrow, Grace was gentle, sensitive, and solicitous. She almost whispered when she spoke to her because she thought her loud voice might break something else on her fragile friend. Grace loved to brush Sparrow's hair while they sang songs. Although Grace knew the words to Tess's songs, she didn't understand them. Sparrow sang *"The wheels on the bus go round and round,"* and Grace loved it!

Sparrow loved to read to Grace and Grace loved hearing her voice the characters in each book. As soon as Grace could read, they took turns making the printed word come alive.

Their favorite pastime, however, was putting on plays. Playing "school" would have been foreign to them as neither had ever attended one. Gus had a raised stage built in the playroom with red velvet tasseled curtains that could be opened and closed. Glittering gold and silver stars hung from the stage ceiling at different levels.

They had trunks full of costumes, wigs, and makeup that they put on each other, and they practiced and practiced for the big performances that they occasionally gave. A red and white popcorn machine with wheels provided the perfect treat during every show.

If Sparrow had broken her ankle, Grace would pull her on stage in a red wagon with a special seat. If it was her wrist, she would cut the costume to fit over the cast. When Sparrow wore a back brace, Grace tucked the costume snugly at her sides as she sat in a wheelchair. "You look beautiful, Sparrow. You don't even have to put it on," Grace assured her.

After Grace and Sparrow sang, acted, and told stories to their captive audience consisting of Tess, Gus, Teddy and the Boys, the girls were worn out and retired to Grace's king-size canopy bed.

Those were the nights of reflection. No one wanted to party or do what they did best—behave badly. Instead it was a dose of reality. They felt little Sparrow was not long for this world and, unfortunately, they were right.

The news came after the first set of a Chicago concert. Gus pulled Kyle aside. Sparrow had been hospitalized with a severe case of viral pneumonia. She had been under the care of Kyle's concierge doctor because of a virus and a cough that made him cringe because he was afraid another bone would be broken in her brittle body.

Tess urged Kyle to forget the show and take the jet and fly home immediately. One of the roadies could fill in, she said, as many of them were talented musicians. She would explain everything.

Kyle was so scared. If intuition was real, he didn't like what he was feeling. "Can Gracie come with me?" he asked. "I don't think I can do this alone."

Tess had never spent a night away from Grace. What he was asking was huge! As she was shaking her head, "No," Gus was nodding "Yes."

She looked over at Grace. Big earphones adorned her head as she watched a Disney movie. "What if the plane crashed?" Tess thought. Waves of guilt washed over her. She had a healthy little girl and Kyle was facing a parent's worst nightmare. She knew she had to say yes.

Gus gathered up Grace and all that it took to entertain her through a two-hour concert. He explained to her that Sparrow was not well and had asked her to come home, to help nurse her back to health. Grace jumped at the chance.

Tess clung to her before they departed. Grace hugged Tess, then took Gus's hand and never looked back. Gus promised to keep Tess informed every step of the way.

Kyle, Gus and Grace arrived at the hospital very late, because of the length of the flight and the one-hour time difference between Chicago and Atlanta. Grace was allowed to poke her head in the hospital room and blow a kiss to Sparrow, who was as white as the sheet that covered her. Sparrow seemed half asleep but whispered, "Gracie, Gracie, Gracie," and smiled at her little friend.

Grace whispered back, "You sleep now, Sparrow. I'm going to take care of you. I love you."

Sparrow fell asleep in the hospital bed. Kyle slept beside her in a chair with his head on her mattress. Grace fell asleep, wrapped in Gus's arms on a sofa in the waiting room. Someone had draped a blanket over them as they slept.

And then everyone woke up...except Sparrow. She was gone.

By late morning, everyone was back from Chicago. Tess immediately called Doris and Ruben and they came right away.

Tess needed help to understand. For the life of her she couldn't comprehend why this had happened. Why would the Lord take an innocent eight-year old child from this earth and leave murderers, rapists, and scumbags? She needed to be reminded that He had a plan because at that moment she was pissed! Really pissed!

Grace couldn't help overhearing conversations and became more and more anxious with each snippet.

"Open coffin...child...sad."

"Natalie...cremated?"

"Sparrow...buried...Atlanta?"

Doris was a true believer who loved the Lord Jesus Christ as her personal savior. She told Grace, "The Lord loved Sparrow and never wanted her to suffer or be in pain. He called her to be with Him. Her time on earth was short but you will be with her again someday and live together forever in eternity. "

As best she could, Doris attempted to explain death to Grace but nothing could console the confused and heartbroken child.

"But when is she coming home?" sobbed Grace.

"She *is* home, child," said Doris.

Sometimes, even if you know something is going to happen, you still don't prepare for it. It's as if you think if you don't confront it, it will go away. No one was prepared to deal with death, especially Sparrow's.

Apart from Gus and Teddy, no one had any family to speak of. There was no family plot where Natalie could be buried and a beautiful monument with an angel on it be erected. There was no family member who would tend to the grave and place flowers in the cemetery on special occasions. There was no family Bible where Natalie's death could be recorded.

They didn't know what to do or how to say goodbye. Gus would have to make a plan. He rescheduled an upcoming concert and cancelled all appointments and prior commitments. He hired a launch and this motley crew sailed out onto the huge lake, a hundred miles from Atlanta, where his family had spent many summers.

As they approached the middle of the lake, everyone stood numb. No one wanted to remember and celebrate Sparrow's life because they were unable to stop mourning her death. Gus silently scattered Sparrow's ashes over the water as Kyle and Grace clung to each other and sobbed. Finally, Doris said, "It's comin' up a cloud. We best move on in."

And then everyone came home...except Sparrow. She was somewhere in the wind.

Everyone handles grief in their own way and although they were there for each other, it was hard for anyone to reach out. Tess, sullen and uncommunicative, never took off her sunglasses. She seemed uncharacteristically distant and angry.

Kyle was inconsolable. He looked like he'd been "rode hard and put up wet." He took to drinking, which everyone knew was not the answer. Gus and Teddy were considering an intervention but he finally started to sober up when it came time to perform.

As for Grace, well, part of her childhood ended. At a tender age, she had lost the only friend she had ever known and probably the best one she would ever have. After the boat trip, she went to the playroom stage and closed the red curtains around her. She put on her headphones and cried herself to sleep on a pile of costumes she had turned into a pallet.

Tess went looking for her and found Teddy in his suite. "Teddy, where's Gracie?"

"I don't know," he said. "I thought she was with *you*."

"No, no, no, she's not with me," said Tess, and she began to scream Grace's name over and over.

All hell broke loose as they searched every inch of the penthouses. When they finally found her, they all wanted to hold her and never let her go.

Instead Tess, Gus, Teddy and the Boys all laid down with her under the stars, on the tutus and costumes of taffeta, lace and ruffles. They closed the curtains and remembered Natalie, their little Sparrow.

Only time could begin to heal their hearts...and it would take a lot of it.

19
The List

Although a little rough around the edges, Tess was a lot smarter than she ever let on. The Boys, not so much. She reminded you of someone who couldn't *speak* a foreign language very well but understood everything that was being said. She was also a good judge of character with an innate sense of pinpointing personas. She just naturally knew if someone was full of it or if they were free of pretense and deceit.

Grace had developed a keen and almost uncanny ability for reading people as well. She knew when they needed a hug, and if she sensed trouble, knew when to make herself scarce. Doris often said, "Grace is an old soul."

Grace was Tess's "Mini-Me," except Grace was often the one who appeared more adult-like. There were many times when her maturity was called upon.

Teddy was honored when his sister asked him to give her away at her wedding. After his dad passed, he became the surrogate head of the family. They all knew they could depend on him and he never let them down as a role model, even if he did work for a rock star. His values could not be compromised and he tried his best to set an example for his brothers and sisters and especially the Boys in the band.

They had all been invited to the wedding but knew from past experience they could not attend. Tess was adamant that it was the "bride's day" and she didn't want to spoil it by taking attention away from her. She sent an extravagant gift with a handwritten note and left it at that.

Since Teddy had become part of the "family," he was seldom away for more than a week and, if he was, then Gus was always there. Teddy cleared everything with Gus and left for the long weekend. "Send pictures, Man!" they all yelled as he left.

Unfortunately, Gus's favorite uncle on his mother's side died the same weekend. Gus knew he had to be there for his mom but was sick about leaving Tess, Grace and the Boys. Tess was not too happy about it, either. She hated feeling so dependent, but she was so used to having her posse around that her heart sank when she heard the news.

Gus had a serious conversation with the Boys before he left. With both Teddy and Gus gone, there would be no one to clean up after them. True, their lawyer was on a retainer—and on call— but that wasn't the point. Gus pleaded with them. "Could you just manage to stay out of trouble for two nights?"

The Boys had looked at Gus like they were deep in thought, formulating a response. They really wanted Gus to give them the answer. As Gus nodded yes, they assured him by saying, "Oh, yeah, we're cool. We got this."

When Gus told Teddy that he would be out of town as well, he said he hoped they didn't end up in jail for doing something stupid. Teddy sighed, "At least you'd know where they were."

Grace overheard Gus tell Tess and the Boys, "I'm going to make a list for all of you and if you follow at least half of what's on it you'll be OK." Gus hoped he sounded convincing because he really had his own doubts. With a heavy heart, he started his journey.

Obviously, no one asked *him* to send pictures.

It seemed odd at first. They all kept looking over their shoulder. They were so used to being called out for doing one thing or another or trying to get away with something that they actually missed being chastised like children. It had become a game, so now where was the fun?

The first night, without adult supervision, they all got together and jammed in Tess's penthouse. Normally, these get-togethers were creative and fun with singing and dancing but tonight it just seemed forced. They missed Teddy's baritone voice and the rich harmony of Tess and Gus. Lately, Gus and Grace would also make music—their voices were perfect together. Even further evidence, for Grace anyway, that they were in fact related.

"Relatives have better musical harmony," her tutor told her.

That night, they did something they had never done before. They went to bed early. The cat was away but the mice didn't play.

As always, Grace was up early. She found the list meant for Tess and the Boys on the dining room table and decided to make Gus proud. She would ask her mom and the Boys to do everything Gus had suggested on the list, not just half. She found her green clipboard and attached the list to it. She decided she would use her pink pom-pom pencil to check off each item. The six-year old was taking charge.

The list started like this:

1. Wake up Tess.

"Yikes!" Grace thought. "This would not be easy. Mom was a heavy sleeper and had been known to be a little grumpy in the morning."

2. Wake up Boys.

"This would be easier. They always love when I jump on their beds and tell them stories."

3. Eat.

"This would be the easiest! ROOM SERVICE!"

Grace tackled breakfast first. She set the table for five and then used the hotel phone in the penthouse. She pressed "Dining" and asked for the chef. She was put right through to Pierre as they were "best buds."

"*Bonjour, mon petit chou,* are you calling for a pimento cheese and bacon breakfast sandwich?" asked Pierre.

"No sir, I am preparing a surprise for Mom and my Boys. Can you suggest something for breakfast?" she asked.

Many times, Grace had heard Gus ask for wine suggestions with certain meals and she loved the way he was always pleased with the result. "Excellent choice," Gus would say. She was not going to take any chances. This was a special meal. A first, in fact, as she had never seen any one of them ever eat breakfast.

Next, she would wake up the Boys. She really wished that she had time to make paper invitations. They would have liked that.

All of them came into Tess's penthouse for the "big surprise," plopped down on the overstuffed white sofas and promptly fell back to sleep.

Mom would be the challenge. Grace entered her room and saw her in one corner of the huge California king bed with a black eye mask on. "Tess," whispered Grace as she gently touched her arm.

"Gus, baby, is that you?" moaned Tess. "Come here. Gimme me some sugar."

"No, Mom, it's me, Grace."

Tess bolted upright. "GRACE! GRACE! WHAT HAPPENED? IS EVERYTHING ALL RIGHT? WHERE'S TEDDY? WHERE'S GUS? WHAT...WHAT'S GOING ON?"

"Everything is fine, Mom. I've got Gus's checklist and a surprise for you." Grace showed her the list and, sure enough, Tess was the first line item.

"OK, I'm awake. Now let me go back to sleep."

"But you'll miss the surprise, Mom," said Grace in an uncharacteristically whiny voice.

"OK, OK, where is it, Gracie Girl?"

The food had been delivered and the Boys were slumped in the huge white upholstered wingback chairs that surrounded the dining room table. They all looked a little edgy—like they were experiencing nicotine withdrawal. The staff was waiting to remove the covers keeping the eggs benedict, asparagus, and stone ground grits hot, all at the same time.

Tess followed Grace to the dining room. Grace was holding the clipboard and the pom-pom pencil and looked rather official. "Oh, isn't this nice," said Tess with as much enthusiasm as she could muster.

Tess sat at one end of the table and Grace at the other. The covers were lifted and a mountain of food was before them.

Before lifting her fork, Grace announced:

1. Wake up Tess. Check!
2. Wake up Boys. Check!
3. Eat! Check!

Grace informed them all that her tutor had said that breakfast was the most important meal of the day. Tess murmured, "Note to self. Fire tutor."

After the first bite, Grace exclaimed, "Excellent choice!" just like she thought Gus would. They all cracked up. More than one of them thought maybe Gus *was* the daddy.

Since they were all up, they decided to give number 4 a shot: Practice. Tess spent the day composing at her grand piano while the Boys developed some new music for songs she had already written. They were actually motivated and productive, at least for the rest of that day.

That night, Tess, Grace, and the Boys were all in the Boys' penthouse watching movies in the "playpen," a custom-made U-shaped upholstered sofa that was enormous. It was really meant for lounging and not for sitting.

Grace was with them because she said she needed to stay up to make sure number 8 could be checked off: Cigarette Butts Out on Balcony. Tess let her, because staying up late one night wouldn't hurt her. She could sleep in the next day.

At 2:00 a.m., they all heard the private elevator door open to the foyer connecting the two penthouses. In walked Gus, looking a little weary but happy to see them. Instead of flying back in the morning, he had spent the last six hours driving to Atlanta.

Tess flew off the couch and ran to him like a lover would. She put her arms around his neck and, as he held her, he kissed the side of her face and whispered something in her ear.

The Boys actually blushed. No one had ever seen them so intimate before. There was definitely some passion in that embrace. The Boys thought for sure they would lock lips at any moment.

Instead, Grace, who was also happy to see him, joined in the hugfest. She successfully cut the sexual tension, which would, at any other time, have been an embarrassment to Gus and Tess. Gus was pulled into the playpen, whereupon Grace regaled him with the stories of what had ensued as a result of the checklist.

The Boys had behaved for about 40 hours straight and were now ready to PARTY! Even though it would soon be daylight, they thought, "The night is still young."

After they left, Grace handed her clipboard and pom-pom pencil to Gus and said, "Your turn. I'm tired." She got on her scooter and rode to her suite in the other penthouse.

20

That In-Be Tween' Stage

*L*ike Tess, Grace loved to sing and play the piano by ear. But her favorite instrument was the violin. Tess had read that left-handed children had a better chance of success with the violin and so introduced it to her by hiring the best teacher in Atlanta.

She was four when she performed in her first recital. After bowing to the audience, she turned around, faced the wall, and performed her piece. Upon completion, she turned back around to the audience and bowed.

It was her first and last recital. She may have inherited her Mom's musical ability but not her propensity to perform in front of an audience.

That was OK with Tess. Although she could never imagine any other life for herself, she knew it was not for everyone. She was pleased when Grace continued to practice and play the violin for her own enjoyment.

Tess loved performing but knew their lifestyle had a negative side. Grace had seen so much in her short life and not all of it was pretty. Although Tess attempted to shield her from that side of rock 'n' roll, it was ubiquitous when they were on the road. Alcohol and drug abuse were rampant. Grace had seen way too many "girls" get sick, pass out, and be taken away in ambulances.

As a "tween," Grace was not judgmental. If anything, she felt sorry for the "girls" who threw themselves at the Boys. Apparently, "the Boys had smiles that made their panties fall off." She knew that some of them were true fans, but that most just wanted to be around fame and fortune.

Grace was intrigued by their tramp stamps, multiple piercings, and distinctive hairstyles. She liked to experiment and copy their dress styles of ripped jeans, designer T-shirts and colorful kicks. Tess would let her braid beads and feathers into her hair and occasionally allow "wash out" hair color. Grace even had rub-on tattoos that she loved putting on her arms and neck. Tess thought of this as a stage Grace was going through and humored her.

The "girls" who followed the band thought that Grace was adorable. They also knew that one way to get closer to the Boys was through Grace. For a while, Grace loved the attention and felt important. And then, one night, amid the activity and commotion before a concert in London, thirteen-year old Grace was harassed by one of the "girls," who had no idea who she was.

"YOU! SKANK! Yeah, I'm talking to you! How did you get back here? You need to get your skinny arse out of here 'cause no one wants to shag that! Why don't you come back after you've grown some of these," she said, slapping her ample chest.

Grace raised both her hands in a stop gesture as the girl continued to approach her. Petie, who had been tuning his guitar, saw the encounter but could not hear the conversation. He saw Teddy talking to security, so he decided to intervene.

"What's going on?" he asked, looking only at Grace. Despite this, the girl answered him. "Petie, remember me from last night? Remember, at my uncle's party?"

Petie ignored the girl and continued talking to Grace. "You OK?" He put his arm around Grace—he could tell she was visibly shaken.

The girl was incredulous. "But, Petie, what about us and last night?"

"There *is* no us," he said as he turned from her and guided Grace to the VIP Room backstage.

Grace felt sad and confused. No one had ever been that mean to her or called her those names. "I think she thought I wanted to be one of your girlfriends, Petie. I guess she didn't know we were related."

As Grace entered her teens, her infatuation with the "glamour" of rock and roll took a serious turn. She had always seen the darker side but was just starting to really understand what was going on and all of its implications. The reality of it all was disturbing, to say the least.

She assumed that the "girls" were always rescued and given help when they behaved badly or made poor decisions. But as she grew older and learned more, she began to understand how difficult it was, if not impossible, to reverse some of the behaviors and the decisions.

Addiction was the scariest and something you lived with forever. Tattoos could be removed by lasing, but it was an expensive, lengthy, and extremely painful procedure. Ear gauging and body piercing sometimes left disfigurement, which required surgery to reverse.

It was no wonder that Tess had a hard time just getting Grace to pierce her ears.

21

A Teen in Transition

To Tess, Gus, Teddy, and the Boys in the band, Grace would always be "Baby Grace, Gracie Girl, or Gracie." To everyone else she was becoming a beautiful young girl. She looked like Tess's little sister who just happened to act older.

For a recent performance, Gus had hired a new roadie named Trey when one of the regulars had some "personal issues," which was code for a stint in rehab. He was young but had experience with another band and came highly recommended. He was "a good Southern boy" who was taking a "gap year" before starting college.

While Trey was on a break, he noticed Grace listening in the wings. He had no idea who she was, but she was hot and so was he. He wandered over to her and started up a conversation.

Because of the loud music, they stood close to each other in order to be heard and were looking quite cozy when Tess first noticed. "Who in the hell is that?" she demanded, to no one in particular.

Tess quickly got Gus's attention and then by jerking her chin toward Grace with her eyebrows pulled down together, Gus knew what she meant. Tess didn't want a stranger talking to Grace, especially after the London incident. For her part, however, Grace was enjoying the attention from someone who looked about her age.

"Trey, you're needed backstage," Gus said firmly as he approached the two.

Gus followed Trey back and told him in no uncertain terms that Grace was barely in her teens, and, as Tess's daughter, was way off limits.

Trey was apologetic. "Hey man, I'm sorry. I had no idea. I know not to even look at anyone under eighteen!"

At the break, Tess demanded to know from Gus who Trey was and why he was talking to Grace. Gus explained everything and said that it was all an innocent misunderstanding.

Grace looked at Tess and rolled her eyes. "We were just talking, Mom. Can't I just talk to a boy?"

Tess responded in a furious whisper. "He is no boy! He's eighteen and you're fourteen. He's a man and he does not need to be flirting with a child! You could both get into a lot of trouble!"

Grace had never responded well to anger and raised voices. Tess could tell she was pulling back, so she tried a different tack. "Look, Gracie, I am just trying to protect you from all of this," she said, circling her hands in the air. She tried to sound calm.

Grace shook her head. "That ship has sailed, Mom."

"Who says stuff like that? Hey, I'm a cool mom, but I also need to keep you safe!"

"*Cool* mom? I wouldn't know because I don't *know* any other moms. I don't know anyone my age!" Grace lashed out with such hostility that Tess was left speechless. She turned and started toward the stage for the final set.

As Grace watched her mother walk away, she finally admitted what she had known for some time…she was lonely in a crowd.

Part 2

Grace

22

The Literature Lover

The Children's Hour

By Henry Wadsworth Longfellow

"Between the dark and the daylight,
When the night is beginning to lower,
Comes a pause in the day's occupations
That is known as the Children's Hour."

As a child, when I read the opening stanza of this poem, I thought it was so sad this father only had an hour each evening to spend with his daughters. I had no idea what it meant to hold down a job and be away from your family every day so that you could provide for them.

I was with my mom every day. In my whole life, I had spent only one night away from her—less than twelve hours—and during that time, I had lost Sparrow, the only friend I had ever known. That experience probably made me cling to the comfort zone of "my family." I wanted to be with them every day and night to make sure no one else would be taken away from me again.

Mom made sure that our life was full, busy, and creative, and that each day was always different. For someone who had lived a large part of her life out of control, she sure knew how to control mine. She had "learned" from her poor judgment, shocking behavior, and dreadful decisions and was not about to let me relive her life of regret. Turns out, though, that everyone needs to experience life in their own way and as much as we try, we can influence, but not develop the mental and moral qualities of another person's character.

I needed space to experiment with my own life in order to become an adult. I needed to learn from making mistakes and poor decisions. Or...I could live like the Boys and never grow up.

In "Ulysses," Tennyson says, "I am part of all that I have met." If that was true, then who was I? I had never known anyone except people employed by my mother or the staff at the hotel.

So how was I supposed to know how anyone truly felt about me? Did they tolerate me and use me? Did anyone really care about me besides Mom, Gus, Teddy, the Boys, and Doris and Ruben? I really wanted to know—or thought I did. What I wanted was affirmation. In retrospect, maybe I should have joined a church where apparently there was an abundance of it.

I had been protected and loved and loved and loved. Can you love someone too much? Can you stifle someone with love so that they feel they can't breathe? I needed to come up for a reality check and maybe some air. I needed some space.

But my mother was as determined as the father in Longfellow's poem who did not want to let go.

"I have you fast in my fortress,
And will not let you depart,
But put you down into the dungeon
In the round-tower of my heart.

And there I will keep you forever,
Yes, forever and a day,
Till the walls shall crumble to ruin
And moulder in dust away."

I needed to be in her heart but not her house.

It was actually Doris and Ruben who convinced Mom to at least consider letting me go to school. Teddy had shared with them some of the recent stories of life on the road. He had always been concerned that I was growing up without friends my own age. With college only a few years away, I needed some kind of segue into real life.

Doris and Ruben, who talked the talk and walked the walk, sent Mom a book of prayers and poems. They placed a sticky note on page thirty-nine and asked her to read it. She read it again and again and again until she had it memorized:

HELP ME. HELP HER.

"I see her as my beautiful child
And cannot bear to let her go.
I see her as a masterpiece in progress
That I don't want to finish.
I see her as fragile and want to
Shield her from pain, fear and failure.
I want her to stay here in my world and be like me.
But I know she doesn't belong to me.

She is unique, a product of two souls.
I can give her love, guidance and encouragement
But it is her choice to take what she wishes.
I cannot always protect her or keep her captive
Because her life is yet to live.

So help me listen to her dreams,
Accept her decisions and embrace her courage.
I want to celebrate her successes and
Help her learn from and not regret her failures.
She is in control of her own destiny, not me.
Help me. Help her. Help me let her go."

Mom responded with a note to Doris and Ruben. In it she wrote, "I don't know what's worse—getting older or getting wiser!"

23

She Wants to Go Where?

The Boys couldn't understand why I would want to go away to school.

"Wait, like she *wants* to go to school? Trust me, no one wants to go to school. Besides, she's safer here with the tutors," said Petie.

JoJo was clueless. "You mean Gracie wants to get up early and get on one of those yellow busses?"

Kyle just bragged. "Our girl knows everything! Just ask her anything. She doesn't need any school."

Gus knew I would go to college but couldn't stand the thought of me leaving any sooner than that. He understood what I was saying but couldn't talk about it or his eyes would well up.

As for Mom, she came up with all sorts of alternatives for me. "Why not go to school in Atlanta? You don't need to be going to a different state."

"And what happens when you're on tour, Mom?" I said. "You love releasing new albums. Who will stay with me? You need Gus, Teddy, and the Boys!"

She sighed. "I also need you, Gracie. We can work this out. I can get you some friends. We can give you some space. Doris and Ruben could come and help out. Besides, we don't have to travel so much."

"I can't talk to you when you're like this, Mom!" Every word came out louder than the one before it. I felt so uncomfortable as Mom and I rarely had "words."

Mom jerked her head in disbelief. "Like what?" she snapped.

"Like a responsible mother making sense!"

"Well, *excuse* me for trying to act like an adult!"

I turned to leave. "It doesn't become you, Mom."

When she talked with Gus later, Mom was inconsolable. "One day, Gracie is trying to be just like me, and the next day, she is looking at me with contempt and giving me nothing but lip."

I really regretted what I said. Mom had always given me nothing but unconditional love...and here I was trying to break free of her control. I didn't know if I was doing the right thing but I knew if I didn't try, I would never know. I wanted to see if I could make friends and be in control of my own life. I wanted that "affirmation."

It turns out, though, that competitive teenagers don't have a whole lot of that to spare.

24
The Prayer

When I was a little girl, I attended a Sunday service with Doris and Ruben. I noticed the way they prayed and upon returning home, I announced to everyone that there were two ways to pray. Ruben prayed with both his hands cupped over his eyes, nose and mouth. Doris prayed with her head bowed and the palms of her hands squeezed together, pointing toward heaven.

"How do *you* pray, Gracie?" everyone wondered.

"I pray like Doris so that I can breathe and peek!" I proudly responded.

I thought of that memory as I waited and prayed for Mom to decide if she would let me go to school. I didn't know if I had a prayer of succeeding, but I knew she was considering it, as the five stages of grief could be witnessed in full force.

I also knew I had not been exactly easy to get along with lately. It was not something that I was proud of, as I was a pleaser and had always tried to avoid conflict.

Mom asked me to come into her bedroom one evening so that we could talk and not be disturbed. I always loved watching movies in bed with her and eating home-made popcorn from the machine in my playroom. This time, we sat on her overstuffed sofa.

"Grace," she said, "I would do anything for you because I love you with all my heart. I want you to know that I hear you and am trying to understand, but I don't want you to leave."

Oh, no, I thought, my heart sinking. *This doesn't sound good.*

She cleared her throat. "Having said that, I *will* let you try this." I threw myself at Mom and hugged her with such ardor that we both fell over onto the cushions.

"Wait, wait, wait," she said as she attempted to corral my enthusiasm. "You must promise me that if this is not working, you will come back and not try to stick it out. And...Teddy Bear goes with you."

I did a double face palm. "Mom, I want to be incognito. I don't want anyone to know our last name or that you're my mother. I want to use your middle name as my fictitious last name. I want to be Grace Mason, period. I can't have Teddy following me around. That would raise all kinds of suspicion."

So, the decision was made and the process began. I was about to learn the hard way to be careful what you pray for. Sometimes it's better to thank God for unanswered prayers.

25

Getting Ready

I had several schools in mind when I began this process. Mom, unbeknownst to me, had also studied the options before acquiescing. She made a list of her requirements and knew which schools she deemed suitable.

She realized that, academically, all of the top schools were acceptable. There was really very little difference between them. Her main concern was my safety and the school's proximity to an airport big enough for our plane to land. She planned on weekly visits.

Mom insisted I learn how to drive a car and a motorcycle before I left for school. If there had been time, I think she would have insisted I learn how to fly our plane. She really meant it when she encouraged me to leave school the minute I was unhappy. She did not want anything—especially transportation—to stand in the way of me not being able to come home.

Teddy and Gus, lifelong learners, had both trained with experts and learned skills for driving in dangerous and deadly situations. They were patient teachers who insisted I learn to drive every vehicle imaginable, including a truck.

Gus also arranged a private instructor for me at a driving school in South Carolina, where I learned advanced techniques that professional drivers utilize.

I loved riding Mom's motorcycle, but my favorite vehicle was our limousine. When I was given a final driving test by Gus and

Teddy, they insisted that the Boys come only because they knew they would be a distraction and I had to learn to deal with that.

Teddy sat with me up front and Mom, Gus, and the Boys piled in the back. The privacy window must have opened and closed fifteen times before the ride was over.

"Chauffeur, could we have a little more air back here?"

"Driver, we are out of tonic."

"I have to pee! I can't help it! Beer makes me have to pee!"

Fortunately, I passed. I remembered everything. I even used my blinker to turn the corner in the parking garage under the condo.

Assured that I possessed these skills, Mom was now ready for me to start the interviewing process. We each wrote down our top three choices for schools, and they ended up being the same although not in the same order.

Like mother, like daughter.

26

The Interview

$\mathcal{M}$om knew she could not be present for the interviews or else she would blow my cover. Suffice it to say, she was not a happy camper but still managed to micromanage every detail.

The plan was that Gus and Teddy would accompany me to the interviews and Mom would wait in the jet with her phone glued to her ear, no doubt.

She rapidly reeled off from the abundant list in her head. "Gus, take copious notes and tell me everything. Teddy, I want you to meet with security and learn all you can about their safety procedures. Advise them that we will spare no expense to make sure Gracie is safe. I'm thinking we need to get one of our men on their team in case Gracie needs extra protection."

I rolled my eyes. "Mom, I think the schools are safe and my guess is that there are plenty of students who are sons and daughters of prominent people. I do *not* want someone following me around," I said, rather petulantly.

Tears welled up in Mom's eyes and she looked away. "Humor me, Grace." Once again, I regretted being so snarky.

As much as Mom did not want me to go, she also wanted me to fit in. She and her stylist studied websites to see what everyone was wearing and how they accessorized each outfit. She had never seen so many sweater sets, preppie pearls, and popped collars. It made her want to gag.

The monogramming really intrigued her as it seemed to be on everything from backpacks to shirt cuffs. She finally decided it must be some kind of laundry issue.

The decision: I should look trendy but classic.

I nixed the pearls and instead wore a silver cross given to me by Doris and Ruben. I was actually comfortable in the dresses and outfits that they had chosen but would have worn whatever they asked. Recently, I had learned to pick my battles in dealing with my mom, and this was not something I wanted to argue about.

No one told Teddy what to wear. At six feet, four inches tall, he looked great in everything but always chose to wear custom-made black suits with white shirts and Italian shoes. He loved beautiful watches and expensive sunglasses and collected them like a hobby. He was trendy and classic without trying.

Gus was also six foot four, but more relaxed and athletic in his style. For the most part, he looked like he should be on the cover of yachting and polo magazines, but for the interviews, he opted for dress pants and a blue blazer. He sure did look handsome.

I interviewed at three different schools and I think they all went well except for one uncomfortable incident at the second school. Gus and Teddy were always more nervous than I was and extraordinarily protective. I was introduced as Grace Mason. No one was told my last name.

Shortly after the interrogation got underway, the interviewer looked at both Gus and Teddy. "And…you…are the father?"

My eyes widened and I looked imploringly at them. My nervousness and confusion were palpable. Everyone else waiting to be interviewed came with their mom and dad, and I wanted to fit in.

At the same time, they both blurted out, "Yes." Because we *were*, for all intents and purposes, family.

The interviewer nodded his head. "Oh, so you're partners…"

Teddy's manhood had been challenged and his Christian sensibilities had been assaulted. He was livid. "Say what! No!" cried Teddy. "What kind of outfit are you running here? I'm not gay!"

Gus burst out laughing and I joined in.

Needless to say, school number two was not chosen.

27

Ready, Set...

While I concentrated on the required reading, Mom planned my departure like a general going to war. The dining room table became command central, with piles of folders with lists, pictures, and ideas of things she insisted I needed. As long as I had my violin, I really didn't care what else she packed for me.

Packages arrived two and three times a day. Opening them like a kid at Christmas, Mom was a little disappointed by my lack of enthusiasm. "Sure, that's nice, whatever" was not the validation she was looking for from me.

She remained undaunted, however, and left no stone unturned. Every *i* was dotted and every *t* was crossed. I even had all new underwear.

In fact, everything I brought to school was brand new. My wardrobe, jewelry, linens, furniture, etc., etc., etc., were all purchased to ensure I "settled in comfortably." I think in the back of her head, Mom wanted everything to stay exactly the same at home so that I could just slide right back in if this "school thing" didn't work out. Shopping also took her mind off my departure.

Everything was then shipped to school in numbered boxes with bills of lading so that we would know what to unpack first.

Well, not quite everything...

The Boys had spent a long time trying to decide on going-away gifts for their Gracie Girl. They wanted something Southern in case

I got homesick and needed some comfort. They knew I would love everything they had chosen and they couldn't wait to see my face. The fact that they had worked so hard on this endeared me to them even more. I loved these guys.

Everything was in one big box with a lid. They had decorated the box with our "family" photos so that it looked like one big collage. I didn't even want to open it as the box was a present in itself.

After a drumroll by JoJo, I began the unveiling. The first gift was two pink plastic flamingos, a mother and baby. The Boys had seen pictures of the school and realized that I would have plenty of lawn in front of my dorm. Doesn't every lawn look better with pink flamingos? Of course, I thanked them profusely and they congratulated themselves with high fives and by opening a bottle of Jack Daniels that they proceeded to pass around.

The next gift was a pink "Carolina Girl" baseball cap that they had purchased on their road trip—in search of the surprise still in the box.

I reached in to find a container of "Barely Legal Firecrackers." The Boys had driven to South Carolina to a store with not only the largest collection of fireworks in the nation but probably the most dangerous. These "babies" had been handpicked.

Again, I expressed my heartfelt thanks and they all beamed. They were pleased with themselves and their gift. Naturally, they wanted to test one out but after some persuasion, I finally convinced them to wait until their first visit to the school to set one off.

My last gift was from everyone. Mom, Gus, Teddy, Kyle, Petie and JoJo produced a compilation of songs that they composed or covered and sang as lullabies to me when I was a child — "Something old, something new, something borrowed and something bluesy."

They had spent the last two months getting it just right and had named it, "Sweet Dreams, Gracie Girl, Love You," because that is the last thing I heard all of them say to me every night of my life before I went to bed.

And unlike any other gift that I have ever been given, that gift melted my heart.

The flamingos and firecrackers didn't make the cut when the last boxes were finally shipped to school. The day I left, I wore the "Carolina Girl" hat and hand carried the hard copy of the compilation of songs in my violin case.

I also took one little firecracker.

28

...Go!

*L*ooking back on the day I left for school, it was one of the best days of my life. Until it became one of the worst.

Mom meticulously planned every minute, wanting it to be perfect. She also reminded me more than once that it was OK to back out of this "school thing" even if I did so at the last minute. Somehow that made me even more determined to go.

Mom and the Boys knew they could not be seen at the school but planned to fly up with me and Gus and Teddy. Three of our roadies would also come, because Mom had planned a big surprise and needed their help.

I didn't dare ask who was coming but secretly wished Trey would be one of them. To my delight, he was. I knew he had slowly won her over. He was intelligent—and a talented musician who shunned the limelight since he preferred to write. Gus and Teddy had continually told her that he was "a good kid," but I guess she had to witness for herself his honesty, loyalty, and respect. He eventually passed with flying colors.

Gus was always the go-to guy and Trey had become the *can-do* guy. There was nothing he couldn't or wouldn't do. He would look at a challenge and then figure something out. But he was also not afraid to admit when he made a mistake and then to ask for advice. If I didn't know better, I would have thought he was Gus' son.

Whoa! Don't even go there. I had always wished Gus was my father, but I certainly did not want Trey to be my half-brother.

Doris and Ruben called to say goodbye and wish me well. They had planned to come with us but then Ruben fell and "blowed out" his foot. I thanked them for the new Bible they had sent me and promised to read the passages they had marked. After hanging up, I giggled to myself. I'd probably be the only student whose desk drawer held a Bible and a "barely legal" firecracker.

Our avuncular New Zealand pilot, Gentleman Jasper—Jazz for short—had the jet ready for takeoff at 9:00 a.m. The ten of us (Mom, me, Gus, Teddy, the three Boys and the three Roadies) all arrived at the hangar a little bit early, much to Jazz's delight. His motto was *Better to be an hour early than a minute late.* The look in his eyes was priceless when we arrived at 8:45.

Apart from my violin case, I had nothing else to stow. The Boys brought their guitars and Mom carried a box of tissues. It seemed like any other short trip we would take at a moment's notice. Except for the fact that we arrived ahead of the scheduled departure.

"Morning, Jazz," I said as I greeted him with a hug.

In his Kiwi accent he replied, "G'day, Miss Grace, let me have a look at you. My, you're so grown up!"

He seemed astonished. It was as if, in his eyes, I had gone from a child to a young adult since I'd last seen him two weeks before. There was a hint of sadness in his voice and a touch of sorrow in his expression that I didn't understand.

But then he smiled and said, "Aren't you just the Bees' Knees!"

Normally, the Boys, who are so easily entertained, would've run with this. They loved Jazz and his Kiwi expressions. They repeated ad nauseam, appropriately and inappropriately, every new one they heard. And Jazz never seemed to run out of new ones, much to Teddy's dismay.

For instance, when the plane checked out, Jazz announced over the PA system, "This is your captain speaking and everything is tickety-boo from the cockpit." The Boys always cracked up because it never stopped being funny to them. They beat that phrase to death to describe anything that went smoothly. They even made up scenarios to use it more. "Hope your day will be tickety-boo, Gracie." Or "Let's shoot off some firecrackers to make this party tickety-boo." It became a game to see how many times they could use the phrase of the day. They thought they were hilarious.

This time, however, after hearing Jazz describe me as the "Bees' Knees" and all grown up, everyone became speechless and solemn. I felt they were all looking at me like I had two heads.

In retrospect, they knew the enormity of what I was undertaking—even if I didn't quite grasp it. Apparently, at that moment, I had a calmness and confidence about me that may have contributed to my newfound look of maturity.

I'm sure they didn't want to face what they knew was coming. I was growing up and, ipso facto, they were too. That was not exactly the problem, though, as they didn't feel any older, they didn't look any older, and they certainly didn't *act* any older.

But, perhaps, it was what they did realize that was most poignant. Things were changing and they didn't want things to change. Few people do. They were stunned because they had no plan for life without Gracie. It seemed to them that they'd blinked— and I was no longer a little girl.

They knew Jazz was right. They knew, too, that I was becoming a beautiful young lady, inside and out, thriving in the chaos. As much as I had fit into their agenda, I had also changed their lives—and in a good way. They didn't want to lose me.

The Boys all smiled and agreed. "Yeah, you're the Bees' Knees." It was easier than admitting I really was leaving and nothing would ever be the same.

I beamed at the perceived compliment. I thought they saw me as grown-up and they respected me for my maturity and the bold move I was making.

29

Advice as in Flight Entertainment

*T*he flight to New England was so much fun. The Boys had realized that they had not yet passed on any words of wisdom for me to take into the "real world" and felt compelled to share their knowledge with me. I knew I had to take this advice with caution, as this same trio had often been described by the media as having "copious amounts of disposable income and continuous lapses in good judgment."

But expounding on what they had learned from just a few of the bad decisions they had made was not what they had in mind. It was more like advice. Which—some of it—no one in their right mind would take.

Petie wanted me to remember not to use too much conditioner in my hair because it would go flat if the air was really dry up there.

Teddy stared at Petie and chuckled. "Really, is that all you got?"

Kyle reminded me of how smart I was and how important it was not to study too hard. "You don't want to be boring."

"Yeah, you want to be a riveting conversationalist like Kyle. Don't you, Gracie?" said Gus.

This kind of banter went back and forth as we all enjoyed the playful teasing. Then JoJo suddenly bolted upright. He vigorously shook his head as if a thought had exploded in it. He leaned over toward Mom and whispered in a voice that everyone could hear, "You *have* had *"THE TALK,"* right?"

Mom thought she knew what he was talking about but feigned ignorance anyway. "What talk, JoJo?"

JoJo responded in an audible whisper, cupping his hand over his mouth—just in case I had suddenly become deaf and could read lips. "You know, about protection."

Teddy chimed in. "Say what?" Normally he would make an attempt to monitor the conversations. The Boys had always spoken openly and honestly (code for "crude and rude") in front of me so it was, for the most part, a lost cause on Teddy's part. But this time, he was listening and actually enjoyed watching JoJo squirm.

Everybody had always felt comfortable discussing my life in front of me and now they thought my future sex life was fair game as well. Trey looked a bit uncomfortable but I was curious as to where this was going. Since I had never really had a serious boyfriend, needing protection seemed a bit premature.

Of course, I had been given "the talk" about sex. In fact, I heard it before my first double-digit birthday. Mom believed that children should learn about procreation at an age when they were ready and could comprehend the logistics but would not be embarrassed by it. She thought that if you waited too long, chances were good that a child might hear incorrect information from others and that could be confusing and detrimental.

So, she had always talked openly with me, answering every question on a level she thought I could understand. It was an ongoing dialogue with real-life exposure, if you will. For instance, I learned very early on never to surprise anyone in their suite by opening the door and charging in. I always knocked and waited for an invitation because they could be dressing...or undressing.

After a few more wisecracks, Mom assured JoJo that when the time came, I would know what to do.

JoJo still shared his piece of advice. In an uncharacteristically serious and thoughtful way, he put his arm around my shoulder and said, "Don't let any boy pressure you, Gracie. You got plenty of time."

Everyone nodded in agreement and said, "Yeah, man. Good advice, JoJo."

30

Tailgaiting with Tess

Upon our arrival at the airport, there were three huge black Cadillac Escalades with heavily tinted windows waiting for us. I climbed into the first one with Mom, Gus, and Teddy. Trey was our driver. The Boys all got into the second one. The third one carried the "surprise" that the roadies unloaded from the plane.

Mom announced that we were going to eat lunch Southern style and that is exactly what we did. We drove to the top of a mountain and then down a dirt road to a recently cleared flat area that smelled like fresh cut grass. It was a perfectly clear day so we could see blue skies and green pastures for miles.

As we admired this little bit of heaven, Trey and the Roadies went to work. Mom had planned the finest tailgate known to man, complete with music and my favorite Southern cuisine.

Under Mom's guidance, Trey and the Roadies got the music started, the easy-ups assembled, the chairs out, and a long table set with silver and flowers. A workstation was set up with a gas stove to heat the she-crab soup, warm the hushpuppies and grits, and cook the shrimp for the shrimp and grits. Unbeknownst to me, Trey had practiced cooking with Pierre, the chef, so everything would taste just the way I liked it.

It was perfect.

After lunch, the Boys brought out their guitars and asked me for song requests. "Anything you want, Gracie Girl? This is your day."

I told them that I wanted to hear some Carolina beach music. The Boys started with *Be Young, Be Foolish, Be Happy* and then the *Hold Back the Night*.

I always loved when the Boys played beach music. Mom and Gus would dance the Carolina Shag. Gus had taught me some steps, but I wasn't a natural like Mom—at times I still had to count some of the steps. One and two, three and four, five, six.

Mom listened to the music and told me that her old manager Jack would have been disgusted. He had always wanted them to act like crazy rock stars and here they were all having fun at a picnic in the mountains singing and dancing to beach music.

As the Boys played and sang *Dancin', Shaggin' on the Boulevard*, Gus looked at Mom and started "reelin" her in like a fish on a line. They met and let their lower bodies move to the music with effortless ease...turn, twist, spin, twirl.

Out of nowhere, Trey came over to me and asked me to dance. I was stunned and could feel the color rise in my cheeks. I looked over at Mom and she just smiled. Trey took my hand, and as the Boys sang *Carolina Girls*, I danced with him without counting...not even once.

31

The Long Goodbye

*I*t was Gus who had to break up the party. No one wanted to see it end, but we had a schedule to keep if I was to get to school on time. We had a short ride ahead of us and then had to unpack boxes once we arrived at the dorm.

Gus, Teddy, and Trey would help me move in while Mom, the Boys, and the Roadies waited on the plane for the three men to return. They would all fly back to Atlanta together minus one passenger...me.

I hugged the Roadies first and then each of my Boys. Mom was handing out tissues like a flower girl throwing rose petals. Everyone was teary-eyed and emotional. Gus was hugging me goodbye even though he was coming with us.

Mom put her arms around me and we walked to the edge of the clearing. We held each other for the longest time and then she said, "Baby, I know you can do this. But if at any time—"

I interrupted her and said in a shaky and not-so-confident voice, "I know, Mom. But I want to try."

Mom couldn't speak. She just nodded as she wiped my tear-filled eyes and then dabbed her blurry eyes with the same tissue. She leaned over and whispered in my ear.

"Love you."

"Love you more," I said.

She shook her head. "Not possible."

We walked together arm-in-arm to the Escalade. Trey and Teddy were already in the front seat and Gus was waiting for me so he could close the door. Mom and I clung to each other until I got in the car and the door was closed. Then we held hands through the open window. As the car started to roll, Mom waved with one hand and covered her mouth with the other.

I jumped back to the third-row seat and furiously waved as I yelled, "I love you!" to all of them until they disappeared behind a hill. I stared out that rear window and never said a word until we neared the school.

Mom and the Boys followed the car until they could no longer see it. Then, Petie told me, Mom threw up. He held her hair as JoJo ran back for the box of tissues. After they helped clean her up, Kyle practically carried her back to the car, and they immediately left. The Boys asked Mom if she wanted them to drive to the school so she could look around, but she declined.

Fame is a double-edged sword. Mom wanted to be with me as I began this new chapter in my life. But she knew she couldn't risk blowing my cover and my chance of living a somewhat normal life.

My safety was paramount. There were many students at the school with bodyguards—students whose parents were diplomats, Saudi royalty, entrepreneurs, and venture capitalists—but no one had a mother like mine. She had way too many obsessed fans and paparazzi who would do anything for a picture.

So, they all drove back to the airport and hid in the safety of the plane like caged birds whose wings had been clipped.

32

This Was Not in The Brochure

"We'll be there in five," announced Trey. I moved into the seat beside Gus, and we held hands across the aisle. Three men and a girl were about to arrive.

We were directed to the bishop's residence to "sign in." This ceremony was recorded for posterity with a photo of the new student signing the book that held every name of those who had attended the school since its inception.

I signed in as Grace Mason. Bishop Gates, headmaster of the school, Father Tony, assistant headmaster, and security were the only people who knew my real identity.

Everyone was cordial, but they were particularly kind to a really good-looking student who arrived after me. William Andrew Abbot III, "Please call me Drew," was a legacy student—his father and grandfather had attended the school before him.

If anything, there seemed to be an unusual amount of attention given to the three men in my company. In terms of looks, they were not mere mortals. They were all Southern gentlemen who were extraordinarily tall and handsome, and had impeccable manners. This did not go unnoticed by the school's female staff and faculty.

I was given my dorm assignment, and we drove to a very old building teeming with ivy. As I stepped out of the car, I could smell mulch that had been recently spread in the flower beds. I carried my violin in my backpack case, and Gus had the folder from Mom with the master list for the boxes. The four of us met my counselor, who actually swooned when she saw Trey. As we walked to my room, she whispered hopefully, "Is that your *brother*?"

When I saw my room, my first thought was, "This was not in the brochure." If Teddy had spread his arms, I think he could have touched opposing walls in this broom closet of a room. Every square inch was covered in boxes. There was no way everything would fit. I wondered if I would become claustrophobic when the door was closed.

Trey whistled in disbelief and then got to work. The first box he opened contained all of my new bras and panties from Agent Provocateur. Apologetic to a fault, he blushed. Before he slit open any other boxes, he checked the master list.

We finally developed a system and worked as a team. Teddy organized and opened the boxes, Gus and I found spaces for everything, and Trey broke down the boxes and carted everything away.

Mom had done an amazing job. Everything was on hangers and in attractive storage containers. She'd even purchased storage units that fit under the bed. The bed, desk, chair, dresser and the small club chair and the ottoman Mom sent pretty much filled the room, but still fit.

The only thing left was to make the bed. It was then that I realized that I had never made a bed from scratch—or even changed one. Sure, I had pulled the covers up, but this was different. Mom had sent a dust ruffle, mattress pad, duvet, duvet cover, and all sorts of pillows and shams.

Again, Trey jumped in, unzipping plastic bags and pulling out bedding. He lifted the mattress and put the dust ruffle on. We both put the mattress pad on and then smoothed out the fitted sheet.

The bed had to be against the wall for everything to fit in the room, so we were trying to make it from the same side and our shoulders kept touching. We kept apologizing for bumping into each other and giggling at the same time.

At that point, Gus and Teddy stepped out. Although Mom was not ready to accept me flirting, even innocently, with a "nineteen-year-old man," they probably thought, "What's the harm?"

How long does it take to make a twin bed? Turns out, a very long time. I felt like I was in a slow-motion movie that I didn't want to end. Every time Trey smoothed out the sheet or the duvet, I also saw the wrinkle and found my hand under or over his as we made the bed that I would sleep in that night.

Finally, Gus and Teddy came back in to take some pictures for Mom. I was really happy with the way everything looked and proud and thankful that she had gone to so much trouble.

I had to grab a bite to eat at the dining hall and then attend a school meeting, so we all knew we had to say goodbye. Gus lowered his voice to tell me one last thing.

"I know you are not allowed to have a car on campus," he said, "but if you ever fear for your safety or need to leave, there is a 'get-away' car parked in the parking garage in town. It's on the fifth floor in space 5-2, your birthday. It's a gunmetal grey BMW with a light grey interior. There is $5,000 in cash under the passenger seat in a black Chanel wallet. The car will open and start only with your fingerprint." Honestly, I was not surprised. Mom had thought of everything and, at that moment of uncertainty, I was glad she had.

Guss glanced at Trey and said, "Give her a hug." Trey put his hands on my arms and went to kiss my cheek. I went left and he went right and we bumped heads. Then I went right and he went left and we did the same thing again. Finally, we met in the middle, and our lips softly touched. He gently squeezed my arms and said, "Good luck, Gracie."

Teddy enveloped me in a big "Teddy Bear" hug. "You remember all those self-defense moves I taught you...and if anyone gives you trouble, you let me know." As he kissed my forehead and told me he loved me, I could feel his wet tears on my cheek.

"I love you, too, Teddy Bear," I said.

And then Gus wrapped his arms around me and I could tell he didn't want to let go. His eyes wet with tears, he repeated the phrase that he had been telling me all of my life. "No matter what happens in life, I will always love you."

I looked up at him. "I love you, too..." I said, and then in my mind, I finished the sentence with what I had always wanted to be true.

...Daddy.

33

Cold Turkey

Maybe I should have gone to camp first—the accommodations would probably have been better. This was all too new, too fast. It felt like everyone—except me—knew someone else and they were all in a real hurry to develop cliques.

The first meeting with the whole school was in the chapel. The counselor gathered all those under her supervision, guided us to the building and then left us to sit with her friends. I found a seat at the end of the row and prayed someone would sit beside me.

Someone did. "Hi, I'm Drew. I signed in right after you."

"Hey, I'm Grace."

Drew seemed to have his own posse of boys, all of whom jockeyed for the seat next to him. Then, an inordinate number of girls smiled and said, "Hello, Drew," as they filed past us and sat down.

I later learned many of them lived in the same communities in Connecticut and the Boston area and their families knew each other from summers on Nantucket and Martha's Vineyard—two venues not exactly part of a rock star's life.

Everyone kinda looked alike. The girls were pretty and perky and the boys were good looking and energetic. They all seemed to enjoy this pep rally that I imagined was like some kind of Pentecostal gathering. They were all so jacked up that I thought for sure they would start speaking in tongues.

Later, I learned they sorta did. This microcosm of students had their own vocabulary, rich in ridiculousness. For example, "mip" was the word for someone with money who dressed like a hippie.

After "Amen," I walked back to the dorm by myself and closed the door behind me. I laid in bed thinking, "What have I done?" I put my headphones on and listened to the compilation of songs that everyone had put together for me.

Gus and Teddy had sung *Ms. Grace* and Mom and the Boys had covered many of my favorite songs. There was even an old recording of Sparrow and me singing *Twinkle, Twinkle, Little Star*. Sparrow sang each verse but left out the last word and I filled it in. At the end of the song, I told her, "I love you, Spawwow."

"I love *you*, Gracie," she said.

Finally, in her beautiful voice, Mom sang *Amazing Grace*.

I was starting to look at my mother through a different lens. I don't think that I ever really appreciated all that she had done because she made everything look so easy. She was talented, capable, and accomplished, and many lives hinged on her ability to perform. I took her for granted and rarely thanked her or gave her credit for anything. In fact, lately, I delivered more thinly veiled insults than compliments. But she never complained. Mom had a well-hidden kind heart saved for the ones she loved.

I glanced at my watch. Everyone would be back home in Atlanta by now, and I knew the first thing they would see was my surprise for them. Before I left, I had put my own homemade gift on the round table in the foyer. It was a clear glass jar with a lid that I had wrapped a ribbon around and made a bow for the top.

I called it a "Memory Jar." I had cut up little pieces of paper and written memories and quotes on each one. I wrote things like:

Disneyland on my half birthdays
Snow Days
"Courage is the power to let go of the familiar."
        — Raymond Linquist

I thought if they missed me they could reminisce. The thing was, though, it was me who was so lonely and missed everyone so much. I had told them that I needed space and that it would be better if we didn't call and text every day but now I was regretting that decision. The day had started so good, but now...

I reached for my phone and started texting with my head under the covers. For some stupid reason, I felt that if I did it that way I wouldn't be breaking my own rule.

Mom, are u awake?

Within a second, she responded. *Yes, of course. Thank you, thank you, thank you for the Memory Jar. I will keep it forever!*

Just wanted to say sweet dreams. I love you, Mom. And thank you for everything."

Sweet Dreams, Gracie Girl. Love You. And then in capital letters, *PLEASE KEEP IN TOUCH.*

I fell asleep listening to my music and thinking about Mom, Gus, Teddy, the Boys and...Trey.

34

Structure May Be Overrated

I inherited Mom's work ethic, so I threw myself into the schoolwork. It was interesting and challenging in the sense that there were deadlines. Being homeschooled, I had always worked at my own pace. Now I was required to attend class, join in discussions, and work within a curriculum. At times, it was exhausting.

Much to my dismay, I also had to take part in a sport. At one time, I had read about a school that allowed you to give up smoking as a way to fulfill the physical education requirement. That was not the case at this school. So, I was forced to participate in some kind of physical activity. I chose fencing only because I liked the uniform and it was an indoor activity.

In my spare time, I continued to play my violin and began writing songs. I pictured Mom writing, and each time I sat down to compose, I felt connected and comforted by the knowledge that we were joined in this way.

In the dorm and all around campus, I could hear Mom's music being played. Sometimes, I wanted to proudly exclaim, "Hey, y'all, listen! That's my mom!" But I knew I would have to admit that I was Tess's daughter and I would never know what it was like not to live in her shadow. I was determined to find my place at this school and maybe even thrive. But, first, I had to acknowledge there were many things I had not been exposed to and learn how to understand and deal with them.

For instance, competition at school was huge. In my former world, I had tried to become a better violinist and a more knowledgeable student for my own benefit. But here, in my new world, everyone was involved in a cutthroat contest where the ultimate prize was acceptance to a prestigious college—not to mention being recognized for your achievements in daily chapel before classes.

And along the way, competition also reared its ugly head for popularity, attractiveness to the opposite sex, and acceptance in the school orchestra to name a few.

I realized that I had grown up with team players—not competing *prima donnas.* Everybody around me had always worn many hats and was willing to jump in and help. Gus had "character radar" and seemed to always hire good people who came and went for a variety of reasons but were never fired. This was a whole new world.

I knew that I possessed some traits from our life on the road that would always be a part of me and hopefully serve me well. Mark Twain said it best, "Travel is fatal to prejudice, bigotry and narrow mindedness." My problem was that I thought everyone shared those hallowed truths. I had so much to learn.

35

Deidre (dee druh)

I desperately wanted to make friends...or *a* friend. I had met many of the other students but had not really connected with any of them yet. In my loneliness, I chose to ignore Twain's words of wisdom. I began to attach reasons why I would not want to be their friend anyway. I pictured petty, pretentious, or petulant stamped on their foreheads and wondered how they saw me. Different? Distant? Dour? I hated being secretly judgmental because I knew better.

And then it happened. I needed a break and decided to take my violin and walk to the music building to play in one of the practice rooms. I arrived at the same time as another girl whom I recognized from two of my classes. Given all the students who were always around her, she seemed pretty popular. Since there was only one room left, I told her to go ahead and take it.

Instead, she asked, "Do you want to practice together?"

Deidre was very talented and played in the school orchestra. I had never played with a cellist and just hoped I could keep up. We each took turns suggesting pieces to play and our hour was up before we knew it. When she said, "Let's do this again," I was all for it.

Deidre's dorm was right next to mine so we walked back together. She was from Connecticut and, like me, was an only child. Unlike me, she had known many of the students before she arrived at school because of mutual family and friend connections. "It's almost incestuous the way many of these people run in the same circles," she said.

I told her that I also ran in a circle in Atlanta but I was sure it was not anything like the one that she was talking about. She laughed and seemed to like that comment, though why, I don't know.

As we parted she said, "See you tomorrow." I said, "Yea, see you tomorrow."

I walked to my dorm smiling. This was the first time that I had had any fun since I arrived.

Deidre was easy to talk to and didn't seem petty, pretentious, or petulant. She reminded me of a puppy who had not quite grown into her paws. She was a pretty girl, whom I'm sure would become a beautiful woman. She was tall with long blond curly hair and dark blue eyes.

I liked the way she seemed confident and open-minded. You could tell that she had someone like Gus and Teddy in her life who instilled in her good manners and respect for others.

The next day, Deidre came into class with a group of girls and chose to sit beside me. When some of the other students filed in they smiled and said hello to Deidre and actually said, "Hello, Grace." I didn't even think they knew my name. I was beginning to learn what it was like to be popular by association.

After class, Deidre and her friends left en masse. When she reached the door, Deidre turned around and smiled at me.

I wanted to stamp "real" on her forehead.

36

The Groupies

Because of my past experiences with the Boys, I could spot a groupie from a mile away. Deidre wasn't a celebrity, but to many of the other students on campus—groupies, if you will—she might as well have been. She was the sort of girl who was so friendly and natural that everyone gravitated toward her.

Two girls in particular, Tate and Judith, followed her like lemmings. Both were smart and attractive and seemed nice. I wondered, though, why Deidre attracted these girls like magnets.

"Please call me Drew," Deidre, and I were in one class together with the Lemmings. Drew and Deidre seemed to have a really nice friendship—their families were close and there were a lot of memories and inside jokes that they shared. They felt comfortable hugging, elbowing each other, and giving friendly shoves. They acted like I thought a brother and sister would.

A class project was announced and we were asked to break into groups of two and three. I knew that Drew and Deidre would work together and the Lemmings would probably team up. I would just join whoever was left in class.

To my surprise, Tate was angling to be with Deidre and Drew and would have happily thrown Judith under the bus. Instead, I heard Deidre say, "Grace is already working with us. Sorry. Let's plan on next time."

I smiled at Deidre, and Drew and mouthed, "Thank you." Tate's eyes narrowed ominously, but she managed a patronizing smile at me.

The class broke into their groups and we all moaned when we were told that the projects were due the first of the next week. The coming weekend was the first one since school started that we were allowed to leave campus. There was no way these projects could be completed without some of the work being done over the weekend.

As we were being dismissed, Tate came over to the corner where we were sitting. With her back turned to me, Tate said to Deidre, "Deidre, my Mom just texted and I have three tickets for you, me and Drew for the concert in Boston this Saturday. The three of us can go and we can stay at my parent's condo. Won't that be fun?"

"Oh, wow," said Deidre, with an apologetic tone. "If only this stupid project wasn't due. The three of us are going to have to work at my house this weekend or we'll never finish it."

"You mean *she's* going to your Greenwich house?" asked Tate.

Deidre nodded. "Yeah, we closed Nantucket for the season."

"Well, I guess I'll just have to invite someone else." Tate turned and left in a huff.

Drew shook his head in disgust. "Can she get any ruder? I'm sorry, Grace, but all I can say is, 'Like mother, like daughter.' She is *such* a social climber."

Deidre looked at Drew and then back at me. "She's not *that* bad. You just don't want to be on her bad side."

If facial expressions and body language were any indication, I already was.

37

The Limousine

om et al. were ecstatic to learn that I had made a friend and had been invited to her home.

Almost every time I phoned, Mom put the phone on speaker so that everyone could hear. I was calling a little more often now that I was somewhat happier. I hated to call when I was sad and lonely—I didn't want to choke-up and cry because I knew it would break their hearts. I also knew that they wouldn't hesitate to fly up.

They all—Mom, Gus, Teddy, the Boys, *and* Trey—had already flown up each week since I had been at school. Their visits had been brief but, I must admit, a lot of fun. Each time, they would bring a surprise for me.

The first one dealt with my woeful living space at school. They actually had architectural plans drawn up for an addition. They all chimed in and took turns explaining how this metamorphosis would take place:

"At first we thought about a balcony?

We realized we were not thinking big enough because it would have to be accessible all four seasons.

Then we thought prefab. In the still of the night, we could have a hydraulic crane stealthily attach your new all-glass bullet-proof wing to the building.

Then during the day, like prisoners trying to escape to the outside world, we would slowly dig out the brick and mortar wall from the inside, and, in no time, the addition would be part of the room. Voila!

We also wanted you to have your own bathroom but that would mean we would have to run plumbing. Someone might notice that.

What do you think?"

Another surprise concerned my physical education class. The Boys thought fencing was so cool that they decided they wanted me to teach them even though I had barely begun. They arrived in full uniform: jacket, plastron, glove, breeches, socks, shoes, mask, chest protector and sleeve, and brought one for me. They carried real swords that I thought for sure Gus would never allow.

They just looked adorable.

We all went out on the tarmac and I taught them the few offensive and defensive moves that I had learned. Their favorite part was jumping into position and forcefully announcing, *En garde* (On guard), *Etes-vous pret? (*Are you ready?), and *Allez* (Go).

Jazz, our pilot, was called by the control tower and asked, "Are those people fencing near your plane?"

With each visit, Mom hoped I would come to my senses and return with them but as tempted as I was, so far, I had held out.

Mom asked me about Deidre and Drew and I knew she would do a background check on them. I wondered if their families attempted to check out my family. I'm afraid they would come to a dead end and that would concern them even more.

I knew Deidre's mom was a community volunteer, whatever that was, and her Dad was a lawyer. Come to find out, Gus was familiar with Deidre's Dad. After Kyle lost Sparrow, he was in a bad way. He got into a car after he'd been drinking and had crashed into a stop sign. That's what you call irony.

No one was hurt, but the whole incident was caught on tape. Given his loss, Gus wanted to help Kyle with this dilemma.

Deidre's father was one of the most experienced, qualified, and successful attorneys in the nation when it came to DUIs. Gus had consulted with him and was able to work things out. I guess there is such a thing as "six degrees of separation" and we really all are connected in one way or another. I don't think, however, this qualifies as "running in the same circles."

On Saturday morning, "the car" was sent by Deidre's parents to collect Deidre, Drew and me. I could tell that Deidre was fascinated by the fact that I was not impressed by her limousine and driver. It actually was almost exactly like ours except our bar has brown liquor and beer and theirs held soft drinks. Also, their chauffeur kept the privacy window closed and ours was always open unless the Boys were playing with it.

I was impressed, however, by her long crushed coral rock driveway and the English manor house at the end of it. The driveway began after huge ornate iron gates opened magically. Well, maybe it wasn't magic—there were security cameras everywhere. Then, the very long driveway stopped and a loop to the house started with a huge fountain in the middle.

Out of two massive mahogany doors stepped a smiling man and woman and what appeared to be an equally-smiling maid, cook and butler. Defending DUIs must be a lucrative business.

Everyone hugged and kissed Deidre like she was the prodigal daughter they had not seen in years. Her parents were also delighted to see Drew and asked about his family. I was introduced and welcomed by Deidre's parents and the staff, all of whom said they were happy to meet me. I felt like I had stepped into an English BBC saga and had just been greeted by part of the family and staff of Downton Abby.

We were whisked inside for lunch at the dining room table. An arrangement of fresh cut flowers adorned the center of the white-clothed table. The silver and crystal sparkled as it was set and reset with each course. If this was lunch, I couldn't imagine what dinner would be like.

Both her parents had graduated from our school and loved reminiscing about the good old days. They told us "scandalous" (actually funny) stories of old friends whose nicknames (Bitsy, Muffy, and Ollie) reeked of money and prep-school affiliation.

The conversation wound around to law as Deidre said it would. "My Dad just loves his work!" We discussed defending people and how sometimes "the letter of the law" and "the spirit of the law" became blurred. *Could he be an ethical lawyer or was that an oxymoron?*

After lunch, Deidre took us on a tour of this very old house and told us about her family history. There were rare books, antiques, original paintings by famous artists—and framed family photos of long-gone relatives—everywhere.

I thought about my family history. I didn't even know who my father *was* let alone my grandparents or great-grandparents. Mom never talked about her parents. It wasn't until I was a little older and started really listening to the words in some of her songs that I realized many were about her life. I learned my family history of alcohol abuse, neglect, and mistreatment in poignant songs that touched...and *broke* my heart...all at the same time.

I was beginning to understand why everyone wanted a piece of Deidre and her family. Her mom was lovely, stylish, and gracious, and seemed interested in everything that was said. I wondered how Mom would fit in here—if she would feel threatened or uncomfortable. Mom *did* like clean surfaces and there wasn't a tabletop in this whole house that wasn't covered in exquisite memorabilia. Actually, I knew she would be fine. She always managed to relate to people — rich or poor, educated or not.

Deidre's dad was witty, charming, and funny, and seemed to know a little bit about everything but not in an obnoxious way. He would be great on Jeopardy.

The whole family wore their wealth well.

They had this incredible home and also a summer place on Nantucket. I know everyone at school didn't live like this but there obviously were many who wanted to, at least for a weekend. I was fairly sure Tate and Judith fell into that category.

From the balcony off Deidre's bedroom, I could see that the limousine was still parked in the driveway. I told Deidre and Drew that I knew how to drive a limousine and asked if they wanted me to teach them.

Deidre and Drew had only ever driven golf carts and thought it was a brilliant idea. Deidre's dad said it was OK as long as the chauffeur sat beside the driver and we drove very slowly.

I started first and duly impressed the chauffeur by pointing out several techniques I learned from Gus and Teddy that he didn't know about. He had not had training in how to escape crazed fans but the knowledge was transferable to terrorists as well.

He was also astounded that I could perform a perfect three-point turn in a tight situation without touching the pristine lawn. I held back showing him my "J" turn or "Reverse 180" as Teddy called it. I was afraid he'd lose his chauffeur's cap, and maybe even his lunch.

Deidre went next and she was a natural. Drew not so much, as he was the hesitant one. Deidre's parents watched from opened

French doors on an upstairs balcony. With all of the car windows and the moon roof open, we took turns going round and round the loop, down the driveway, and then back up to the loop, and around to the front of the house. Deidre's parents could hear us laughing and squealing and her father thought it was hilarious. We heard him shout, "Great driving, Deidre!"

After Deidre and I had dressed for dinner, we went down to join her parents in the library. I heard Deidre's mom ask her father about *my* parents. "I know Deidre said Grace's father is out of the picture, but what did she say her mother did?"
We stopped outside the door.
"I think Grace said her mother was a musician based in Atlanta."
"Do you think she plays with the Atlanta Symphony?"
"Probably...I guess so. In any case, I like this girl's spunk."

At dinner, we discussed situational ethics, and then devoted the evening to our project. We felt good about the result.
We all slept in Deidre's playroom in sleeping bags. It was my first sleep over party. It was a seminal moment for me. On Sunday, we all hugged goodbye and arrived at school in late afternoon.
The chauffeur insisted on driving.

38

The Bully

I was starting to settle into the rhythm of what was becoming my life. Looking back, I wondered what I thought it would be.

Did I think a change of venue would mask who I was? Well it didn't, because that's just geography. Did I hope that being around different people would give me lots of tolerant friends and a sense of belonging and membership? Well it didn't, because many students were ultra-competitive and in some instances downright mean.

All I knew for sure was that I missed my family and TessWorld. I longed for the witty banter, the Boys' shenanigans, the belly laughs and the hugs that we gave so generously to each other.

I missed my stuff because everything here was all so new. I wished I had taken some of the things that I prized the most, like some of the books Gus had given to me. For every birthday, he presented me with a book that had inspired and influenced him during his lifetime. Each was inscribed with beautiful sentiments. I read every one of the books over and over and learned so much from them.

Fortunately, I had Deidre and Drew. Although I met more people and considered some of them friends, I always preferred to be with and spend my free time with Deidre and Drew. And I knew they felt the same.

I wondered if Drew told Deidre who was with me when we signed in on the first day of school. Gus, Teddy and Trey would certainly be memorable and an anomaly. Neither of them had asked about it and I didn't offer any unsolicited information. I accepted them and they accepted me.

I knew Tate and her minion, Judith, continually vied for Deidre and Drew's attention. I really didn't care. I also knew that Tate and Judith seemed a little bit too preoccupied with obtaining details of my background, and that I cared about because it made me nervous.

It was Drew who reluctantly shared some of the venom that spewed from Tate's mouth. He could not stand "that snake," and felt compelled to warn me. He stood up for me and righted every wrong.

Tate made fun of my manners ("Who says 'Yes, sir' and 'Yes, ma'am' unless you're a Southern hick?"), the fact that I was homeschooled ("She's probably some kind of born-again Christian"), and my violin case ("That old thing looks like it's been around the world and back"). That last one was actually true.

In retrospect, most of her comments were not harmful to my body but they were hurtful to my soul. I didn't know why Tate was attacking me, so Deidre helped me understand. "Tate wants to be my best friend," she said. "And she thinks you're Drew's girlfriend. She wants you gone because *she* wants him."

It had nothing to do with looks, personality, or money. Who knew that bullying was an equal opportunity offender? No one and nothing was immune or safe from it and the reasons were endless.

Both Deidre and I knew Drew was never going to be my boyfriend. Even though we never discussed it, we both knew he was not interested in either one of us, even if the rest of the world didn't. But we loved him and we were willing to perpetuate that myth.

"Guys," I said to Deidre and Drew, "Do you think I could figure out how to deal with her in a better way?"

"Are you kidding me!" exclaimed Deidre. "You do not need to learn how to become a better victim! She needs to be stopped!"

Most people go along with bullying, afraid to defend the victims lest they become one of them. But Deidre and Drew were not most people. And they were helping me realize...neither was I.

39

The Spy

As a child, I had never visited a library. Teddy and my tutors would take me to bookstores, but we mostly ordered everything.

The school library, built on a hill, overlooked the lake. It was the highest point on campus and my favorite building. The library had floor to ceiling windows that let in lots of light. It was far more contemporary than the rest of the buildings, which were dark and drafty and covered in ivy and probably bugs! I loved looking over the campus more than walking under the canapé of trees. I had only lived in a tall building with light-filled rooms so I was used to seeing life unfold at a distance.

I was told that years ago, after the building was finished, the books had to be transferred from the old library. Everybody on campus formed a line from the old library to the new one and each book was passed to the next person in line until the old building was empty and the new one was full. I think that is part of the reason why this building had such a good feel about it. It was built brick by brick...and then book by book.

One night, Deidre, Drew and I were studying in the library in some lounge chairs next to the stacks. Drew wadded up a spitball, threw it at me, and then feigned ignorance. I threw it at Deidre and did the same thing. She couldn't figure out where it originated and we all cracked up. We were tired and a little punch-drunk.

"I wish we had a car we could jump into and just leave this place!" Drew lamented.

"Maybe that can be arranged," I shamelessly boasted.

Deidre squinted at me. "Do you have a car, Grace?"

I smiled, shrugged my shoulders, raised my eyebrows and gave the impression that maybe I did, maybe I didn't, without saying a word.

"Let's make our escape plans," Drew whispered conspiratorially. We all began to giggle.

Unbeknownst to us, Tate's minion, Judith, was standing in the stacks listening to our whole conversation. Judith never heard me say, "Yes, I have a car," because I hadn't responded out loud to Deidre's question.

In the next moment, Judith stepped out from the shadow of the books and said, "Oh, hello...I didn't know you were here. I'm going to call it a night. See you later."

We knew Judith was probably on her way over to Tate's room to report what she had heard. Drew and Deidre just shrugged it off, but I didn't. Although I really *did* have access to a car, it was not on campus—which according to the rules was not allowed—and I did not want to have to explain it.

The next day, I received a formal email from the Honor Council that made my heart sink. I sped-read the highlights—or lowlights as it were:

"It has come to our attention ...
Non-academic violation concerning car
Meeting tomorrow morning 8:15 AM
Before Honor Council
Faculty, staff, students
Determine if evidence exists
Action to be taken."

I wanted so much to call Mom and get it all straightened out. But I didn't want her to be seen as doing something wrong. She'd left the car because she was mainly concerned about my safety.

I couldn't believe Judith had done this to me. I had hardly even spoken to her, ever! I should have known. She was, after all, Tate's best friend. It reminded me of an old Japanese proverb: *When the character of a man is not clear to you, look at his friends.*

I wasn't afraid...but I was worried.

40
Honor Council

After reading the email, I immediately met with Deidre and Drew. They were furious.

As we all hugged, I shared with them how surprised I was that Judith would do this. I had expected it from Tate but not her.

They were sure Tate was behind it because she was one of the student representatives on the Council. They refrained from telling me how she loved the power and took joy in intimidating anyone, even if they were accused of a minor infraction.

"OK, we have to make a plan," said Deidre. "It is my belief that they have come to a conclusion from hearsay and now they are searching for evidence. It's a fishing expedition. We have to fight fire with fire because Tate's bullying has got to end."

As soon as our classes were over, we rehearsed answers to possible questions. Deidre and Drew never asked me if I actually had a car, on or off-campus, and I never told them one way or another. I don't think they really wanted to know because that way they could honestly deny any knowledge of a car. I think Deidre's father would have called that "plausible deniability."

They impressed upon me that I should never lie but I could answer "creatively." Deidre cautioned me. "Remember, be careful because if the crime doesn't kill you, the cover-up will."

The next morning, as Deidre and Drew walked with me to the meeting, several students wished me luck. The news had apparently spread like wildfire that I had to go before the Honor Council. As we continued to walk across campus, groups of well-wishers continued to join us and upon our arrival at the meeting we were about fifty students strong. I felt humbled.

The meeting began at exactly 8:15 a.m. Judith and I sat in wooden chairs about ten feet away from a very long rectangular table. Eight people were seated behind the table: four faculty members, two staff members and two students. Tate was one of the students.

Deidre's, Drew's, and my English teacher, Miss Meyers, was among them. That gave me hope as she seemed like a decent person. Everyone introduced themselves and then the questioning went something like this:

Miss Meyers began, "Judith, could you please tell us what you heard."

Judith replied, "I heard Drew say he wanted to leave campus in a car. Grace said she could make that happen. Then Deidre asked Grace if she had a car. Then Drew said, 'Let's escape.'"

Miss Meyers then asked, "When Deidre asked Grace if she had a car, did Grace say she had a car?"

Judith said, "I didn't hear her response but if Drew said let's make escape plans, then I think she must have said yes."

Miss Meyers asked, "But did you hear her response, Judith?"

"No," said Judith.

Miss Meyers then turned to Grace.

"Grace, did you tell Deidre and Drew that you had a car on or near campus?" asked Miss Meyers.

"No, Ma'am, I did not," I answered.

"Do you have a car on or near campus?" Miss Meyers asked.

"I have never seen or driven a car owned by me or my family on or near campus," I replied.

"If we searched your room, would we find car keys?" asked Miss Meyers.

"No, Ma'am, you would not," I responded. "But, please, feel free to search my room."

"Well, all right, Grace. I think there has been a misunderstanding. You are allowed to go now. We are sorry for the inconvenience," said Miss Meyers.

"Just know this will be on your permanent record," said Tate, her voice dripping with disdain.

Miss Meyers immediately responded. "Tate, this will not go on Grace's permanent record or any other record. It is not your decision to make. You have just overstepped your bounds." Then, she turned to Judith. "I would like to see *you* after this meeting, which is now adjourned!"

On her way out of the room, Tate—who treated every faculty member like they were subservient to her—turned to face Miss Meyers. "I don't care what you think. It *should* go on her record!"

Because the meeting had been so brief, all the well-wishers were still waiting outside the building. Even though I felt like the only person in the world who had ever been bullied, there were many I knew who had not managed to escape Tate's tentacles.

When I came out smiling, I was immediately hugged by Deidre and Drew. Everyone wanted in on it and our hug morphed into what looked like a huge rugby scrum with cheering all around. The bells pealed, signifying that morning chapel was about to begin, and we all went on our way.

I saw Tate quickly leave the building, but I didn't gloat.

I felt exonerated but also dishonest. I succeeded because of the letter of the law but not the spirit of the law. I had answered the questions truthfully but in actual fact, I did have a car that was accessible to me off-campus.

True, Tate was trying to hurt me again and probably get me thrown out of school, but did that situation give me the right to defend myself as I did? Was this a question of situational ethics? Did the end justify the means? Was there a greater good that would come of it? Would Tate and Judith stop bullying me or was I just trying to rationalize my performance?

All these secrets were beginning to weigh heavily on me. I thought of Sir Walter Scott's words: "Oh, what a tangled web we weave, when first we practice to deceive." I longed to bare my soul and wished I could tell Deidre and Drew everything about me.

41
The Audition

The weather was getting cooler and the leaves were beginning to turn colors.

Walking around campus always presented a challenge whether it was the distance I had to walk or the weather I had to walk in.

Neither Mom, the Boys, nor I were really outdoorsy or athletic. We were pretty much "inside night people" who preferred a hermetically-sealed environment with the temperature hovering around 72 degrees year-round.

Here, I felt like I had to prepare for every climatic change because each hour could be different. I could wake up to fog and as the day progressed, I could see showers, wind and maybe sunlight. I dreaded the snow, which I knew would come, and the dark, cold, shorter days of winter.

Every day started with chapel in a somber, ornate church. The inside walls were covered in dark wood paneling and the only natural light came through the colorful stained-glass windows. We sat in assigned seats on benches of hand-carved wood. You always knew when someone was missing.

Coming out of chapel one day, I noticed a poster detailing information on auditions for the orchestra. I had not joined any clubs and was warned by my academic advisor that I needed some extracurricular activities, "Grace," he had said, "You are academically gifted, but you need an edge. Why don't you join my cycling club?"

I decided I must look more athletic than I am because riding around on a bicycle for pleasure was just not going to happen.

The next day, during a torrential downpour, I walked to the auditorium in the musty-smelling music building, toting my violin under a sturdy golf umbrella. I signed in and waited in the lobby with the other students. Listening as each student came out of their audition, I figured out that there were four people making the decisions—two faculty members and two students who were in the orchestra.

I was the last person to audition. When my name was called, I walked into the auditorium from the back lobby and could see the backs of the heads of the four judges sitting in the audience section. I was asked to climb the stairs to the stage and begin my piece. I took my violin from the case and was poised to begin, when...

I looked down at the judges and saw her. There was Judith, one of the student judges, staring right back at me. I felt total despair, but decided that maybe this was what I deserved. What goes around comes around—the consequences of my actions had caught up with me.

I imagined that Judith was relishing the poetic justice of this whole situation. She would finally get her deserved retribution when she voted against me.

I silently screamed in my head. "You won!"

I put my violin back in my case, descended the stage and practically ran toward the lobby without saying a word.

"Wait!" yelled Judith. "Come back! Audition. I can be fair."

I looked into her eyes, the windows to her soul, and saw... nothing. "Could she be fair?" I wondered.

Or was she afraid that if she didn't give me a chance, everyone would think she was a bigger bully than Tate? At least she could say I was given an opportunity to audition and that I was just not good enough.

Or was I just paranoid because of my guilt about the car?

Or was she lying, and had no intention of being fair?

I guess we all lie to each other in one way or another: exaggerating, fabricating, bluffing, telling half-truths, polite lies, lies of omission, and cover-ups just to name a few.

Drew and I were both lying.

I was learning the hard way that I must be true to myself. I was ready to come out and say: "Yes, I am Grace *and* I am Tess's daughter."

Drew would need more time.

I auditioned. Two days later, the list of orchestra members was posted. My name was not on it.

42
The Confession

During the next weekly visit from everyone, the surprise was a puppy. She belonged to Trey's sister and was a tiny, adorable Lhasa Apsos. Her name was Rosie and she loved having her tummy tickled.

On the flight up, the Boys had taught her some commands and tricks that they had her proudly perform for me. One was putting a tiny treat in front of her and saying, "Eat." She gobbled it up and we all clapped and agreed how smart she was.

Another trick was holding a treat above her head so that she would have to stand on her hind legs to retrieve it as we said, "Dance." There seemed no end to what they could teach her and what she could learn, we all joked.

We were having so much fun when suddenly I burst into tears. "I miss y'all so much," I said between sobs. Everyone fell silent and surrounded me with love.

"I can't be someone I'm not," I said, still blubbering. "I am proud of all of you and I want to put pictures of y'all in my room, just like Deidre is proud of her family or else she wouldn't have all of those dead relatives in picture frames." I was barely making sense but went on and on and on...

JoJo was distraught. "Wait...we can get you pictures of relatives."

Petie started to jump in, but Gus put his hand on his shoulder. "Boys, let's let her talk," he said.

I continued my lament as I blurted out that some of the girls were mean to me and made fun of my violin and my manners, and were jealous of my friendship with Deidre and Drew. I told them the whole story about the Honor Council and my audition: "I was the last one and I was so upset because that bully Judith was one of the judges, but she said she could be fair," I said, between hysterical sobs.

Mom was very emotional. "That car is for an emergency! You shouldn't have to answer those questions. And they should just accept you in that stupid orchestra for all I'm paying them!" She looked at Gus. "How much am I paying them, Gus?"

"A lot," he replied.

"Mom, it doesn't work like that here. This is not the kind of place where everyone can participate and get a trophy. It's very competitive," I said.

She wrapped her arms around me and we hugged and rocked. I told her, "I want to stop pretending. I want to be your daughter." She held me tight and said, "I know, Baby."

I'm sure Gus and Teddy would have liked to be able to "fix it," as men tend to do, but there was nothing anyone could do. I *did* feel like a ton of weight had been lifted off me, though. Talking about this, as women tend to do, and letting go of all of this pent-up emotion, was liberating.

Some of the things that I was so upset about seemed to lessen when I shared them and said them out loud. I had made a bigger deal about some things than I probably should have. Being with family allowed me to put everything into perspective.

When I finally calmed down, I told them about some of the more positive things that had happened. "Some of my dormmates and I had a little kitty follow us back to the dorm. We were able to find a home for the little guy with our housekeeper, Annie."

I also told them all about Deidre's driveway and her elegant house and how much fun we had that weekend. They were so proud that I taught Deidre and Drew how to drive the limousine. I showed them some pictures that I had taken on my phone.

We talked about the new album they were working on and then I said that I'd better get back. Mom was speechless—I think she thought for sure I would fly back with them. I didn't, even though I longed for the uncomplicated life of just being Tess's daughter.

Gus told me later that on the return flight, Mom was distraught because she had never seen me so upset. She'd gone into her private quarters on the plane and called Doris and Ruben.

As always, they were the two people in which Mom felt she could truly confide. Humble and sincere, they were as honest as the day was long. And they kept her grounded.

Although they had never attended any of the concerts, they had come to many of her award ceremonies, and, sitting front and center in their church clothes, had seen her perform. Doris had always prayed that Mom would find success and happiness, and since she had, Doris often told her, "My heart is full."

Their needs were modest, but Mom made sure they never wanted for anything. She bought them gifts and gave them money, all the while knowing they gave most of it anonymously to their church.

Mom gave them a shortened version of what had happened and they listened attentively. When she finished, Ruben said, "You know Tess, being a mom is a blessing. Just know that the first forty years are the hardest." Mom laughed so hard that everyone heard her in the main cabin.

Doris said, "You know, Tess, you're only as happy as your most miserable child. Maybe you could do something to make Gracie happy and proud...in front of her friends. I believe you'll think of something."

When Mom hung up the phone, she knew exactly what that wily and wonderful Doris was suggesting.

Put on a concert.

43

The Violin

Mom had become a problem solver and was quite good at it. If she couldn't solve something, she would find someone who could. She had always been privy to problems encountered by everyone in her entourage and made a point of personally getting involved to help solve them. This was one of the many reasons everyone who worked for her was so loyal.

Having her own daughter with a terrible problem—being attacked, bullied, and snubbed—deeply affected her, and she could not let it go. She had spent way too many years of her childhood cowering in the shadows and attempting to avoid attacks and abuse from two people who preferred drinking to parenting. She had learned how to appear absent even when she was present—don't talk unless you're spoken to, eat what's put in front of you, and never ask for anything.

No one was going to hurt me the way she had been hurt if she could help it, so she felt compelled to retaliate. Somebody was going to have to pay.

I later learned from Gus that Mom began planning the concert the night I "lost it" and told them about the debacle with the Honor Council and the orchestra. Her plan was to have me play and sing with her and show the school that I was too good for their stupid orchestra. Mom wanted them to regret their decision—big time.

Although Mom didn't understand why those girls made fun of

my violin, it didn't matter. She was determined to buy me a new one and to hell with them. Mom wanted them pea-green with envy when they saw the new violin. She, of course, didn't realize that it was the well-worn violin *case* that was the object of ridicule.

Gus was more than a little surprised when Mom announced she was buying me a Stradivarius. She had told him, "I need to buy Gracie a new violin. I want the best, a Stradivarius. I want to give it to Gracie at the concert for her half-birthday. Here is what I found so far. Can you help me?"

Gus knew better than to try to talk her out of it but wanted Mom to, at least, hear what he had to say. He was concerned she was taking this too personally. He thought that I seemed to have fought my own battle in my own way and didn't need her interfering.

He told Mom that neither he nor she had any control over whether Judith and Tate would be nicer to me and that what she was planning would likely add an even bigger reason for them to be envious of me. Whatever they did, there was no guarantee that I would feel better. Another of his concerns was that I might refuse to perform. Then what? He reminded Mom of my first and only violin recital.

Gus's greatest concern, though, was pragmatic—having a multi-million-dollar violin at school. If someone tried to steal it, I could get hurt. Plus, she would not be able to insure it—there were no locks on the doors of the school.

But, he also knew that once Mom's mind was made up about something, she rarely changed it. It broke her heart to see me in pain and she had to know that she had done everything in her power to make it right—whatever that turned out to be.

Mom later admitted that this had not been her finest hour. But I knew, even then, that she couldn't help it. She was always fiercely protective of me and sought to get back at anyone she held responsible for my unhappiness. Her "mama bear" instincts were on steroids.

44

Meeting My Modern Family

I was now ready to celebrate who I really was, but it wasn't something that I wanted to announce in morning chapel. I was conflicted as to how I should go about it.

In a way, I wanted to say to Tate and Judith, "Oh, by the way, my mother is Tess and I was homeschooled because I spent my life traveling around the world and having a wonderful time."

Of course, that would be totally boastful, which I knew was not right. It was my bravado concerning the car that got me in trouble in the first place, and I did learn my lesson.

I thought it would be a good idea to start small. During one of the weekly visits from Mom et al., I would introduce all of them to Deidre and Drew and maybe have a bite to eat on the plane.

I had asked Deidre and Drew to meet my family and they were looking forward to it. They had no idea who my mother was and I thought it would be much easier to surprise them than to explain it. I thought after they met everyone, there would be fewer questions.

I had met both of their families and I think they were curious about mine. Drew's family had seemed to really like me. They lived in a lovely old home filled with family heirlooms. It was apparent they were from "old money." I'm sure they thought Drew and I had a crush on each other—they certainly made every effort to encourage it.

Drew's father was a minister, who adhered to a strict interpretation of the Bible and his mother was very active in their church. It was obvious that they were a loving family, but neither Drew nor I was sure how tolerant. Drew's younger sister genuinely bubbled over with joy and enthusiasm. I'm sure everyone thought they were the perfect family.

When we left Drew's home, his parents asked us three times to please come back soon. I wondered what the preacher would have thought if he'd known my mother was a rock star.

When I asked Mom if I could bring Deidre and Drew to meet everyone and have dinner, she was uncharacteristically quiet.

"You do want to meet them, don't you?" I asked.

"Of course, Baby," she said. "Do you think they'll like *me*?" Her own insecurities were beginning to show.

I made a face. "Mom, they'll *love* you!"

"OK, then," she said. "We'll plan something extra special!"

I could see her re-establishing command central on the dining room table. No detail would be too small that it wouldn't warrant her laser-like focus. She obsessed over what to wear and drove her stylist crazy trying to find the right statement outfit.

She texted me constantly. *What did Deidre's mother wear when you met her?*

I didn't even want to go there. I told her the outfit she wore the last time we were together would be perfect.

Pierre, the chef from our hotel, would cater the dinner and come with them to make sure everything was served at the right temperature. Jazz, our pilot, was asked to detail the plane. He'd already had the carpet replaced where Rosie, the puppy, had peed.

The Boys thought it would be fun to dress like they thought rich people would. It didn't matter that they were worth tens of millions of dollars. Their usual attire was jeans and T-shirts, but they wanted to step it up a notch for "Gracie and her friends."

When Teddy pulled the limo around to drive everyone to the airport, he cracked up. Petie was wearing a tweed newsboy cap, Kyle had a pipe in his mouth, and JoJo was sporting an ascot...over his T-shirt.

After the plane landed in New England, Trey drove to school and picked us up in the Escalade we kept at the airport. Mom and the Boys had become such regulars at the airport that they were now allowed to taxi to a fairly secluded area and not be seen by the general public.

Trey gave me a peck on the cheek, and I introduced him to Deidre and Drew. I know they wondered who he was and where we were going, but they never asked for details.

We continued to the airport and were met by Jazz waiting for us at the bottom of the stairway to the jet. He also gave me a peck on the cheek, and a big hug. Deidre and Drew continued to look confused.

Then Mom, with a huge smile on her face, appeared at the door of the jet. Both Deidre and Drew gasped and stood like statues until I finally said, "Come on. I want you to meet my mom." I leapt up the stairs and gave Mom a big hug and kiss. We turned and looked back down where Deidre and Drew, still frozen, watched from below.

Jazz finally had to prod them. "Get on, then. Up the stairs." They both moved like they had never boarded an airplane before—slowly, cautiously, and trembling with trepidation.

"Mom," I said, when they finally reached the top of the stairway, "these are my friends, Deidre...and Drew." She hugged them each in turn, and as I watched, it occurred to me that she looked like she could be their peer. I introduced Gus and Teddy next and they both shook hands with Deidre and Drew. I never said Teddy was our bodyguard, driver, or moral compass, because that was just the role he played. I was introducing them to my family.

Pierre poked his head out of the galley, blew a kiss, and motioned in some kind of sign language that his remoulade sauce was at a critical point and he would talk later when we all sat down to eat. I glanced at Deidre to see if I could tell what she was thinking. I was pretty sure that Deidre's family never ate with their cook.

The Boys were next. I hugged them all and said to JoJo, who was still wearing his ascot, "John Joseph, you look so handsome and debonair!" He coyly smiled and shrugged his shoulders, looking very pleased with himself. I turned to introduce them, but a very impressed Drew beat me to the punch. "Wow, you're JoJo...and you're Kyle...and you're Petie!"

Everyone smiled and nodded and then JoJo said, "Yeah, and you're Drew!" JoJo had a fifty-fifty chance of getting that one right and a hundred percent chance of making us all laugh.

Once Deidre and Drew were finally able to speak, we all just cut up and carried on like we usually did. Everyone soon fell into a comfortable rhythm. I think my friends—I *did* like the sound of that—were actually surprised at how unpretentious and fun everyone was.

Pierre had prepared an exquisite meal with some of my favorites like crab cakes and fried okra. Normally, Gus would have opened fine wine for a meal like this, but I noticed no one was imbibing. I assumed that Mom had read them the riot act, warning them to be on their best behavior.

It started to get late, and although nobody wanted it, I had to break up the party. We had a curfew and I didn't want to get into any more trouble. As we said goodbye, there were no handshakes this time—only hugs all around.

On the ride back to school, Deidre and Drew talked nonstop. They relived the entire evening and talked about all the funny things everyone said and did. "You look just like your mom!" they said. "She's so beautiful! You could be sisters! How could we not have seen that before?"

Trey dropped us off with a minute to spare. He hugged Deidre and me, and gave Drew a manly hug—a pat on the back and a handshake. Deidre and Drew had had a great time...and, like me, now had a crush on Trey.

Pierre's parting gift to me was a cooler with pimento cheese and bacon sandwiches and a jug of sweet tea. He knew the way to a Southern girl's heart.

45
The Announcement

*A*t the next visit from the family, the weekly "surprise" left me dumbstruck. *Mom had meticulously planned a concert that would take place in fewer than ten days.*

She and the Boys were so excited because they all wanted to do something nice for me...now that I wanted to tell everyone whose daughter I was.

Knowing that the Boys thought it was such a great idea should have raised a red flag right then and there. Any time they had "great ideas," questionable outcomes almost always ensued. Being who they were, it didn't stop them. Teddy described them as "often wrong, but never in doubt."

I knew what Mom was trying to do. She was going to fix things. She had done this all of my life. "Let me make you comfortable. Let me buy you this. Let me take your pain away, etc. etc. etc!" she would say as she made her emotional appeals. She was determined to be the mother she never had. Trouble was, she had enough love and concern for ten kids even though there was only one recipient. Me!

I knew her *modus operandi*—she would want me to perform. Mom knew I was talented and wanted the orchestra to rue the day they had given me a thumbs down.

I knew she had my best interests at heart and I felt I owed it to her to show as much enthusiasm as I could. After all, this was all going to happen whether I thought it was a good idea or not.

146

I became very protective of Mom, and I wondered if the school was ready for her. I knew my peers loved her and played her music continually so that was not the problem. I was most concerned about some of the "holier than thou" faculty members and the administration who seemed very judgmental.

What they didn't understand was that, despite all, my mother was a quiet reflective person with an inquisitive nature. She related to people from all walks of life, which to me was a sign of a very intelligent person. Mom cared about my feelings but one thing I knew for sure—she would say that she didn't care what some sanctimonious hypocrite thought about her. "You can't make everybody like you, Gracie," she often told me. "That would be like spittin' in the wind."

I had questions for everyone. "When the school accepted your generous offer to perform, did they have any stipulations that they wanted enforced?"

"Yes," said Gus. "They asked for a playlist and for Tess to wear appropriate attire." He and I both knew that he would give them a list and then Mom would go and do whatever she pleased. There was no point telling her what she couldn't do—it would only make her want to do it more.

Let me just say that during her performances, Mom never "colored inside the lines." The lyrics to many of her songs were not for the faint of heart. What she considered "harmless sexual innuendo" would be construed differently by some of the faculty members and the administration.

I was shocked that the school was on board with this. It was obvious that the decision-makers had never seen Mom and the Boys in concert.

Then I learned that a capital campaign for a new music building was about to kick off and they wanted Mom to be the first person to see the plans for the still unnamed building. The pieces of the puzzle began falling into place.

46
The Music

*C*ould I get expelled from school for something my mother did? Who knew what could happen at this place!

I knew the concert would be fabulous because Mom's performances always were. Every one was better than the last because she felt that she owed that to her ever-growing and passionate fan base.

Many different types of musicians also idolized and revered her sound because she was so eclectic. Tickets were always sold out because fans and fellow musicians just couldn't get enough of Mom and the Boys.

Mom's music and "sound" continually evolved, but the common thread had been that her music made people feel like someone cared. She wrote poignant and powerful lyrics that were interpreted and retold in the minds of those who heard her sing.

She never told anyone what her songs meant. She just hoped that her music would find a way to touch that place where the heart, soul, and mind meet. Judging from her success, she had found that sweet spot.

As juvenile as the Boys generally were, when it came to their *music*, their focus, collaboration, and discipline were remarkable. No one could ever accuse them of phoning it in or acting like it was a job—they were dedicated to their craft.

As musicians, Mom and the Boys never tired of exploring new boundaries and toying with different genres. They played bone-rattling rock 'n' roll but could just as easily segue into jazz and blues. Their concerts always included the customary tracks that their listeners came to expect. These favorites contained choruses that were not going anywhere once imbedded in your brain and fans loved hearing them again and again.

Their live performances were historic. They fed off the crowds and the energy was explosive. Their goal was to entertain and have the time of their lives while pushing every limit.

In retrospect, it was not the playlist or the attire that I should have been concerned about. It was the behavior on stage that no one had any control over. If experience had taught me anything, it was that you never knew what they were going to do. And *that's* what their fans loved about them.

If the school wanted a new music building, then the faculty and the administration would learn to love it, too.

47

By Invitation Only

The concert was to take place on a closed weekend when students were not allowed off campus. The students, faculty and staff were all urged to attend this important surprise "assembly." They made it sound like there would be some kind of huge announcement, so everybody was curious.

Only members of the school community would be allowed to attend. During the negotiations, the head of the school attempted to invite other heads within the league of schools, along with his family and friends. Mom had said absolutely not, because of security concerns.

Mom knew what he was doing. She was nobody's fool. "Old money" would always give to the school they attended with the hopes of securing a spot for their children when the time came. But schools were always competing for "new money" and that's what Mom was—new money.

The school's headmaster thought he had hit the jackpot—a mega-rich, mega-rock star with a smart daughter. He wanted to gloat. He wanted everyone to know Tess was performing a free concert at his school.

Mom, on the other hand, was determined that no one would have access to the performance just because of someone's status. IDs would be checked and the only exceptions would be people that I invited.

I wanted to include Deidre and Drew's families if they were comfortable with that. Drew was not, but Deidre invited her mom and dad. Miss Meyers, the English teacher who had been very kind to me after the incident with Judith and the Honor Council, was engaged and I wanted her to bring her fiancé. I also wanted our housekeeper Annie and her husband to attend.

I hadn't even met Annie until we were looking for a home for the kitty that followed us back to the dorm. Students were kept on a very tight schedule and I was never in the dorm when it was being cleaned. Annie had seen what we had posted on the bulletin boards around campus: "Adorable free kitty! Shots are up to date and comes with a crate, bowls, toys, food and treats."

Annie wanted the kitty.

The next time I saw her was when I had gone back to the dorm because I was upset and crying after my audition. She was alone in the building and I could hear her voice as soon as I entered. She was singing *What a Wonderful World*, and sounded just like k.d. lang. She stopped when she saw me and we both said, "Hello." I went straight to my room and attempted to compose myself before my next class.

The next day, I found a packet of Sugar Babies, my favorite candy, on my desk. Annie must have occasionally seen the packets when she emptied my trash and had bought some for me because she knew I was sad and upset.

That night I left a note by the pail in the broom closet where she kept all of the supplies. I didn't write a salutation or sign my name. I just wrote, "Thank you." I hoped that it put a smile on her face because she certainly had put one on mine.

48
The Logistics

The logistics of putting on a concert in a very small venue was more difficult than anyone originally anticipated. All the Roadies were required but finding space for what they wanted to do was the challenge.

Gus, Teddy, and the Roadies all arrived at the auditorium and oversaw the construction of huge elaborate white tents. The whole area was then cordoned off with fencing and a gate because nothing says "STAY OUT" like a chain link fence. It was additionally secured with cameras monitored by our staff in a white van. All of the equipment trucks would drive into the tented areas to unpack and set up. Unless you were authorized, you were not able to see anything or anyone.

The whole campus was abuzz. Rumors were flying. Was the President coming? Who else would require that much security?

I was anxious to see everybody. I hadn't seen any of the Roadies in a long time and couldn't wait to catch up. I met with Gus and Teddy and the Roadies briefly but knew any further contact would arouse suspicion as to why I was privy to the tented areas when no one else was.

Although Mom and the Boys appeared to perform impulsively and spontaneously—which the audience loved—Mom always had an outline as to what she wanted to include in each performance. The Boys waited for her cue.

Mom had planned something special during the concert for both Miss Meyers and Annie. She asked me if Drew, a pianist, and Deidre, a cellist, and I would help her out with the surprise for Miss Meyers. I knew she would figure out how to drag me up on the stage. Her plan was really sweet and since Drew and Deidre wanted to participate, I felt I couldn't say no.

Deidre and Drew were even more excited when Mom offered the services of her wardrobe stylist, makeup artist and hair stylist. The three of us met her hours before the concert on the plane, where we had our makeovers. She had several wardrobe options for the three of us to choose from and ideas for our hair and makeup.

Deidre's transformation was amazing. She tended to wear baggy preppy clothes and usually pulled back her long, thick, blond curly hair in a ponytail. Mom suggested she have her hair blown straight but with plenty of fullness. Her makeup was subtle but her blue eyes just popped. Deidre chose a short fitted black dress that showed off the great body she normally hid under sweater sets, corduroys and puffy vests. She looked beautiful. I wasn't sure her parents would recognize her.

Drew looked like one of the band. He totally and thankfully deviated from his polo shirts and khaki pants. He chose ripped jeans and a great T-shirt. Mom suggested he have a haircut and he was so star-struck that he just looked at her like a little puppy, and said yes to everything she suggested. He looked great with a layered cut and cool clothes, but I was sure his parents would probably think he had joined a cult and would insist on an intervention.

I noticed one of Mom's favorite dresses among the options that she chose for me. I picked it even though it was a little low cut. My hair had grown a lot and I decided to get a trim and have it nearer the length of hers. I was really embracing this mother-daughter thing like I had when I was a little girl, and I knew Mom couldn't be any happier.

49

Chas Beau

But the best surprise arrived as the finishing touches were being applied to my makeup. Out of the window, I could see another plane taxiing up alongside ours. I thought that was very unusual and when I questioned Mom about it, she said, "That is one of *your* surprises, Baby."

I could not imagine what she had purchased for me that had to be delivered by a plane to our plane. I was more than curious, but I couldn't rubberneck because my mascara was being applied.

When finally, my makeup was finished, I quickly walked to the door to disembark and there he stood, replete with his red-lined black cape, Chas Beau! I threw my arms around his neck as he carried me into the plane and spun me around.

Charles Robert, otherwise known by his stage name, Chas Beau, had won about as many awards as Mom for his musical talent. He was a yearly regular at The Grammys, which was where they met many years ago. I think out of all the people in the music industry, he was Mom's best friend. They both had experienced difficult childhoods and had bonded over shared secrets of abuse and the shame of feeling they'd somehow deserved it. They had helped each other realize it had not been their fault. Mom thought of Chas as the brother she almost had.

As long as I can remember, every time I saw him, he would take my index finger and make me twirl around in front of him.

He would comment on how tall I had become or how cute my outfit was. This time as he twirled me he pointed to his own chest and as he waved his index finger back and forth, left and right, he yelled, "What's with the cleevaaaage? Teddy, are you allowing this cleavage!" He loved teasing Teddy as he thought he was "just a big ol' prude." Then he turned back to me and gave me another hug. "You look beautiful, Gracie," he said in my ear. I couldn't help but giggle.

He then grabbed Mom and enveloped her in his cape. They kissed European style on both cheeks and I heard her say, "Thanks for coming, Chassy. I may need you *and* some sippin' liquor before this night is over."

I introduced him to my friends and they, of course, knew who he was, too. Chas *was* unique. He not only enjoyed the excesses of rock 'n' roll, he embraced them. He was famous for his outrageous outfits and opulence, but he was also generous with his great wealth—gift giving for him was an art. And he never forgot my birthday.

The first gift I ever remember receiving from him was on my fourth birthday—a midnight-blue, battery-powered Bentley convertible. He had just added a full size one to his car collection and had an exact miniature replica custom-made for me to ride around the penthouses and the hotel ballroom. It had thick lambs-wool carpeting—dyed blue—and dove-gray leather seats embroidered with Bentley emblems. I still have it parked in the front hall closet in the condo.

The last gift he'd given me was an after-hours shopping spree at Neiman Marcus. The store was fully staffed and we had four personal shoppers at our beck and call. I was told to pick out anything I wanted, but he'd also bought things that he wanted me to have. Most of the clothes and accessories still had the tags on them in my bedroom closet back home.

Chas swung around, looking for someone. "Where's my man Gus?" He had a huge crush on Gus and was always trying to promise him anything to entice him to join his entourage. He would swoon and wink and sashay in front of him and Gus would smile and quietly giggle in a masculine way. He was never embarrassed by Chas's behavior or flirting. Underneath all their surface differences, it was obvious the two of them really liked each other and got along well because they were both comfortable with who they were.

And I loved them both in the way a daughter loves her father.

50

The Lead Up

*W*e all drove back to campus about an hour before the concert was to start in big black SUVs with heavily-tinted windows. There were tons of people waiting to get in as we passed through the gated chain-link fence and into the white tents. After we were safely inside, the fence and the tents were taken down, rolled up and carted away.

Mom always liked arriving early so she could do a sound check and get a feel for the venue. It was important that the lights, sound, and stage perfectly complement, but not overwhelm, the music. As always, Gus and the Roadies had done a terrific job organizing everything.

Still, Chas Beau's white Steinway crystal piano, which he insisted on sending up, seemed to take up half the stage. JoJo's drum kit took up the other half. Chas's entourage was also enormous. They were all milling around trying to look and act busy but there was only so much setup for one man and his custom-built piano.

Mom was accustomed to performing in front of tens of thousands of people in stadiums and arenas and although she had seen all of the arrangements on paper, she was still amazed at the small size of the auditorium. She said to Gus, "I could reach out and touch the front row!"

Gus was busy organizing last-minute details. The doors would all be opened at the same time and after the concert, they would stay shut until Mom and Chas Beau were on the road. Teddy and his team had insisted on that for security reasons.

Trey had done a doubletake when he saw Deidre and Drew. The dramatic change in their appearance was eye opening. Deidre was not used to receiving this kind of attention for her looks, but Trey was sincere and respectful. "Y'all look amazing. Good luck tonight," he said.

Then he walked over to me, and said, "For Miss Meyer's song, I will bring you your violin and Deidre her cello...and you look beautiful." I smiled, but I really wanted to give him a big thank you hug and kiss. Actually, I wanted to...well, never mind.

Once the doors were opened and everyone started filing in, the excitement was palpable. The noise level was extraordinarily loud. Unlike a normal assembly where the back rows were filled first, everyone wanted to sit up front. They all hoped to get a better view of what was about to unfold.

Eleven seats in the first row, middle section were reserved with names on them. I was to sit in the middle with Drew, Deidre, and Deidre's mom and dad to my right. To my left would sit Bishop Gates, Father Tony, Miss Meyers and her fiancé, and Annie and her husband.

Minutes before the concert was to begin, Deidre, Drew and I stepped out from behind the stage curtain and walked down the steps to take our seats in the audience. There were hugs and hellos to all of our guests. Deidre's parents were stunned by her appearance and very proud of their beautiful daughter.

Out of the corner of my eye, I could see Tate and Judith seated several rows behind us. Of course, they were front and center. Neither could bear to be left out of anything.

They would soon know my truth. How they would react would be anyone's guess. At first, I wondered, "How will they treat me?" Then I thought maybe I should redefine the question: "What was I going to *do* about it?"

As Deidre had pointed out, I didn't need to learn how to cope. I refused to become a "better victim"—no one has the right to make you feel unsafe, uncomfortable, or unhappy.

I had a feeling they would leave me alone from now on. I decided my mission would be to stand up for any other student they might bully. I knew they wouldn't stop until someone stopped them—I might as well be that someone.

51

The Concert

*O*ut of nowhere someone started slowly clapping and the whole audience joined in. Then someone stood up and everyone else did too, so as not to miss whatever was about to happen on stage. Then some chanting began and the air was filled with, "We are ready! We are ready!" But for *what*, no one knew.

And then it happened. The curtains opened, and there sat Chas Beau at his grand piano playing and singing one of his signature songs that everyone loved and knew every word to. He was wearing giant red sunglasses and red cowboy boots. The crowd went crazy! They were actually jumping up and down and singing the lyrics.

More than a few people were skeptical. "That can't be Chas Beau! That's the best impersonator I ever heard! But it *could* be him with all the security!"

He played two songs and managed to whip the crowd into a frenzy! Just when I thought the energy level could not get any higher, the Boys stepped out and I thought we would have to administer smelling salts to half of the sobbing girls in the audience.

Then Chas and the Boys started playing one of Mom's Grammy-winning songs and everyone started screaming! She ran out onto the stage and in her powerful, perfect voice delivered the best rendition of it that I have ever heard. People were actually hyperventilating.

After singing one more song, she stopped for introductions. When she screamed, "Let me introduce myself. I am Grace's mom but most people know me as Tess. The audience went wild! All eyes were on me as Mom yelled, "Love you, Gracie!" She turned to the rest of the people on stage. "This is my friend Chas Beau." She waited until the noise died down a little and said, "and these are my Boys, Kyle, Petie and JoJo. And this here is my man, Gus."

It felt like an earthquake was occurring because the auditorium seemed to shake with excitement and noise. Everyone was clapping and fist pumping and trying to stand on the seats! I giggled to myself—this was a far cry from the response that last week's string quartet performance had received.

All my fears were alleviated once the concert began. They loved Mom and all the covers and original songs she performed. She looked fabulous in a low cut, skin-tight dress that I'm sure the bishop would not have officially deemed "appropriate attire." She didn't change a thing about her wardrobe and wore what she would have to any other performance. Her only concession to appropriateness was a very long strand of pearls she knotted half way down. And JoJo wore...an ascot.

During the concert, they played songs from just about every genre: pop, country, jazz, soul, blues, gospel and rock, to name a few. At one point, Mom said, "What's up with you guys? You're treating every song like it was your favorite. Sit down and rest. We're not even half over!"

But, of course, no one would. After that, she started moving into the audience, something I had never seen her do before. As she returned to the stage, she signaled to me that it was time for Miss Meyer's surprise.

Drew went up and sat next to Chas Beau at his piano while Trey put out a chair for Deidre. He brought out her cello but *not* my violin. Instead, Gus handed another violin to Mom and as the Boys played *Happy Birthday*, Mom walked over to me with the Stradivarius and said, "Happy *Half*-Birthday, Gracie." Then she kissed me.

My jaw literally dropped open. I looked at Mom and she just smiled. "Go ahead, tune it Gracie. It's yours—we just have to keep it in Atlanta."

As Drew, Deidre and I played, Mom and Gus started singing an old romantic favorite, *The Way You Look Tonight*. They left the stage and came back into the audience where Miss Meyers and her fiancé were sitting. Gus slow-danced with Miss Meyers as Mom danced with Miss Meyer's fiancé. Then Gus and Mom put them together and everyone sat down to watch Miss Meyers and her fiancé dance while Mom and Gus continued to sing. A collective "Awwww" was shared by everyone.

Then Mom switched gears again. She started singing one of her songs and walked over to me in the front row. She pulled me back on stage and handed me a wireless microphone. We sang the song together—she would sing the first part of a verse and I would finish it.

Finally, she nodded for me to do the rest of the song by myself. She walked over to Father Tony and started dancing and flirting with him. The priest, who looked to be about fourteen, turned scarlet. It was way too much erotic activity for someone I don't even think shaved yet.

After that, Drew and I played a piano duet. At the end of it all, I leaned over and kissed him. He looked stunned, so I quoted Ecclesiastes to the preacher's son: "To every thing there is a season and a time for every purpose." Then I whispered, "That should keep the jackals at bay until you're ready to be you."

Chas and the Boys started playing again and then Gus came on the stage with his saxophone and I joined them all with my violin. We started playing the music to *What a Wonderful World*, which was the same song I had heard Annie singing in the dorm the day of my audition.

As Mom had done with me, she went down to Annie and held out a wireless mike. Annie hesitated for a second and then took the mike from Mom, who then wrapped her arm around Annie's shoulder. They swayed back and forth, and the audience—again on their feet—imitated their motion. Mom began to sing the song and after a little coaxing, Annie finally joined her. The juxtaposition of a breathtaking rock star and a matronly housekeeper was striking. But in that moment, Mom and Annie were a divine duet.

At the end, they both sang *I think to myself...* And then Mom said, "What *do* you think, Annie?"

Annie smiled at Mom and sang in her k.d. lang voice, "What a wonderful world!"

The audience exploded into applause.

Mom returned to the stage and started to sing a song she wrote for me just after I was born. Without a thought, I joined her on the stage to sing it with her. Holding the same microphone, with tears streaming down our cheeks, we sang *I Need You* to each other. There wasn't a dry eye in the audience.

No one wanted the music to stop. I knew everyone in the audience would be hoarse the next day from all of the screaming. Mom had performed longer than she had anticipated but I knew she was winding down when she started *Last Chance for Love*, her signature last song. She walked to the middle of the stage and a single spotlight focused on her. You could have heard a pin drop.

The song started in a slow, soulful way and and then she let it rip. Everyone was up and clapping and Chas, Gus and I formed a conga line behind her as we literally danced and sang our way up the aisle and to the door. When we reached the exit, Mom yelled, "Good night, New England!" The music came to a crescendo and then stopped dead, just as the doors to the building slammed shut behind us.

52

Get in the Car!

When we reached the outside, Teddy was standing guard. Mom, Chas, and Gus climbed into the limousine while the Boys slipped out a backstage door. No one inside the auditorium would be allowed to leave until they were all safely gone.

"Wow, that was intense, huh, Chassy—kind of fun, though!" exclaimed Mom as she sank into the buttery soft leather seat and threw the mike she still carried onto the seat in front of her.

"Gus, I think we are ready for some brown sippin' liquor! Fix us some, will you?" He handed her and Chas crystal glasses filled with two fingers of Jack.

"None for Gracie, though. Give her one of those coolers. Get in the car, Baby Girl."

"Mom, I'm fifteen. I can't legally drink," I said.

"What is the drinking age here?"

I rolled my eyes. "The same as it is in every state."

"I knew that," said Mom. Truthfully, I doubted it.

She sniffed. "Get in the car, Gracie. I have a *BIG* surprise for you."

"Mom, I can't. It's a closed weekend and no one is allowed to leave campus."

"I don't care. Gus, go tell the pope we're taking her!"

"Mom, he's not a pope, he's a bishop."

"OK, then, go tell the bishop we're taking her and while you're at it, tell Bishop Tony to come with us. We can show him a good time!"

"Mom, Father Tony's not a bishop — he's a priest."

She shook her head. "Are you kidding me! This is worse than the monarchy and the military!" She paused and then giggled. "But at least those guys have cute uniforms!"

"So, you want the bishop to come with us?" teased Gus as he left the limo and stood outside the open door.

"Hell no! I want Tony!" Mom looked up at me. "Is this about the Strad, Gracie? Because I don't care if you keep the violin here, but we worried about your safety if someone tried to steal it."

I sighed. "It's not about the violin, Mom."

"Then get in the car. I don't want to have to discipline you."

I smirked. "You've never made me do anything."

"What! Help me out here, Gus."

Gus snickered. "Well…you made her brush her teeth."

"I rest my case," Mom said. "Now get in the car!"

Chas jumped in. "Gu-u-u-s! You need to get back in the car, too!"

Gus shook his head. "Chassy, I'm not leaving until I know all of the roadies are out of here."

Chas fluttered his eyelashes. "Can't Teddy do that?"

"No, because he carries the gun and needs to protect y'all."

"Well," said Chas. "I'd be willing to take my chances."

My phone suddenly started ringing. I stared at the phone and then looked at Gus and shrugged my shoulders. "Father Tony is calling me." I answered and held the phone to my ear. "Hello…?"

For the past few minutes, our assistant headmaster had been trying to get past the very large bodyguards. When they'd refused to open the doors for him, he'd asked Deidre for my number.

I listened for a moment and my eyes popped open. I whispered as loudly as I could, "Mom, your mike is still hot! Shut it off!"

Mom's eyes got wide. "Oh, sh—!" She grabbed the mike and turned it off, while all of us stared at her. She looked at us like an innocent child. "What? What did I say? I didn't do anything!"

The audience had eavesdropped on the conversations of the "rich and famous" and they all thought it was hilarious.

Except for the bishop.

53

The Inn on the Lake

Teddy told the bodyguards to let Father Tony out. The young priest's cheeks were flushed with victory and excitement as he approached the limo. I had the feeling he wanted one more chance to see Mom.

With her mike now off, Mom purred, "Come on in, Tony. You are about to have the ride of your life."

Father Tony blushed again. "Oh, no. I can't. I'm just here to tell you that Grace can leave campus. And to thank you because the concert was brilliant and I think you are amazing and beautiful, you know, as a performer and a singer..."

Everything he said was so heartfelt and downright sweet that even I wanted to kidnap him. I knew if he came with us, wherever we were going, he would be shaving by the end of the weekend. But some things just aren't meant to be.

As the limo drove off, Mom filled us in on the big surprise. As a thank you to all of the entourage, she had rented the entire Inn on Woodlawn Lake for an all-inclusive weekend. I was excited because I knew it would be amazing.

We arrived at the lake late on Saturday night but were greeted by the full complement of the staff, all of whom had been sworn to secrecy.

The only people who shared a room were Mom and me—Mom was not about to leave me unattended with this wild and wonderful group of people—although I think many of the rooms would be shared before the weekend was over.

Mom knew that the weather was to be unseasonably warm so she'd had the Harleys sent up along with my riding jacket, chaps, helmet, boots, and gloves. She loved riding in the country in the morning, so we were up and on the road by 10:00 a.m. I always rode with Gus on the first bike. Mom and Trey followed and Teddy rode sweep.

Mom and Gus used to ride without helmets until I started to join them. Now it was all about "dressing for the slide and not the ride." Originally, I was happy about that decision because it was safer. But on that beautiful day, I thought how cool it would be without a hot, heavy thing on my head.

We returned from our morning ride to a sea of white. Everyone wore white fluffy robes and matching terry cloth slippers. "Breakfast Beers," Bloody Marys, and mimosas were flowing. Chas and JoJo were duly robed and deep in discussion over black coffee. JoJo squinted at me. "Haven't I seen that outfit on you before, Gracie?"

I giggled. "Yes, you have, JoJo. You Boys gave me an identical one for my second birthday. I still have it in the same closet with my Bentley."

Chas looked at JoJo and winked. "Obviously, our excellent taste is timeless."

In the afternoon, I thought everyone would gravitate toward the spa but Mom and Chas had arranged for some outdoor activities. It was like camp for adults (and I use that word loosely) with participation trophies and uniforms. "Everyone is a winner," said Chas. "That's how we roll."

I had the feeling that although the day was planned for the whole group, it was especially for me. Mom had obviously discussed my orchestra audition debacle with Chas and they were going to show me how evolved they were in giving everyone a chance to participate but not in an obnoxious competitive way.

The "trophies" were an enticement. Playing a round of croquet, win or lose, entitled you to a watch; participating in a wine tasting earned you an iPad; riding a horse warranted a new TV.

There was one catch. Chas had gone to great lengths buying the proper attire for every activity and wanted everyone to dress the part. So, the white fluffy robes morphed into riding outfits with velvet hunt caps, cowboy clothes with Stetsons, white croquet clothes, boating attire with yachtsman's caps and an abundance of pirate finery with eye patches. As the afternoon progressed, the outfits became multi-dimensional. I saw JoJo, who was supposed to be pirate, gallop by in a white rubber bathing cap with a chinstrap, all the while swinging a badminton racket.

There was music and laughter everywhere. Mom and Chas were the nucleus and sat in lounge chairs all afternoon sipping drinks, laughing, chatting and just taking it all in. At one point, I plopped down beside them.

Chas cleared his throat. "You know, Tess, I never thought Gracie would be interested in performing—you know after the violin recital—"

I let out a long sigh. "Won't anyone ever forget about that recital? It's been over ten years!"

"Hold on, princess," said Chas, turning back to Mom. "Obviously that cute back-turning thing is over. And...after hearing Gracie sing last night...I'm thinking I want her to open for me at my next concert."

Mom jerked her head around and looked at me and then back at him. "Are you crazy! Over my dead body! *You* know what's out there!"

Chas made a face at Mom. "And you don't think she does? Tess, she's been exposed and overexposed and she's turned out just fine. Give her a little credit."

Chas's offer shocked but excited me, and I nodded in agreement. "Yeah, Mom," I said. "Give me a little credit."

As the sun was about to set, everyone gathered around for one last activity. A banquet table and cases of champagne appeared. We were each invited to "saber" a champagne bottle—open it with a sword! After a short demonstration, Trey was first up and of course he was successful. After that, you would have thought participation was mandatory the way everyone wanted to give it a go.

A roaring fire was started in the huge stone fireplace beside the lake. Adirondack chairs and small tables were placed all around it. The stars hung over the lake and the autumn moon reflected on its calm waters. Mom had arranged a Lowcountry shrimp boil for dinner and as we enjoyed good ol' Southern food, fireworks began over the lake. It was magical.

I was sitting next to Trey. Everything was perfect. I thought that I had died and gone to heaven. I could tell Trey wanted to say something, but he waited a long time before he got up the nerve. Finally, he did. "So, you have a boyfriend now?"

I sat up. "What? No! What makes you say that?"

He shrugged. "I saw you kiss Drew. I'm happy for you. That's all."

I was unconvinced about his being happy for me. In fact, I thought he sounded a little jealous. That gave me good chills from the top of my head to the tip of my toes. "Trey," I said, "Drew and I are friends. He's not interested in me…or any other girl for that matter."

"Whoa," said Trey. "I totally missed that!"

"You aren't the only one," I said. "No one really knows. The kiss was to give him a little more time."

Trey reached out his hand and I took it. Eagle-eye Teddy saw this and pulled up a chair in between us. "Would you look at those fireworks! They really are something special."

We all giggled because we knew exactly what he was doing.

It had been a long fun day, but everyone was winding down. I knew I had to be back on campus early for morning chapel but I didn't want the night to end. I had had a lot of time to think—it seemed so long ago that I had yearned for structure in my life. Now I really missed spontaneity.

This life, this crazy weekend of performing and partying was familiar. Structure was not. Sure, everyone could be disciplined when necessary but, for the most part, chaos was normal for us… and I missed it.

In a very short time, I had matured physically and emotionally, and had learned some valuable lessons. One was that you can sometimes be wrong by being right. I think it was right to want my own life and not live entirely in Mom's shadow. But had I left too soon? Should I have waited until college? Then again, sometimes you need to leave home to realize how good you have it. To be old and wise, I apparently had to be young and stupid first.

Mom and Gus said they were going to "call it a day," which was code for me to come with them. Mom glanced over and said to

Trey, "You can walk with us if you want." He jumped right up and followed us into the inn.

Inside the door, Gus turned to Mom and me. "Do you want to take the bikes to school tomorrow? It's a short ride and the weather will be warm." We both said, "Yes," without hesitation.

We said good night to Gus and then Mom went into our room and said to me, "I will see you in exactly thirty seconds." When the door closed, Trey quickly moved toward me and wrapped his hands around my neck and into the back of my hair. He gently guided my lips to his. I took a deep breath and as I slid my arms around his neck, I felt his hands move down my sides and then up my back as he pulled me even closer.

Twenty-nine seconds later, I slipped through the door with a big smile on my very red face.

Mom and I fell asleep reminiscing and giggling about the whole weekend. It had been awesome.

54
The Ride

Everyone woke up early Monday morning for the trip back to civilization. I said good-bye to Chas Beau, the Boys, our entourage, and all the new friends I had made. The four bikes were brought around front and were waiting for us. I rode with Gus again, followed by Mom, Trey, and Teddy.

Trey had the Stradivarius strapped to his back in a custom carbon backpack and Teddy had his revolver strapped to his side. Teddy was not about to let that multi-million-dollar violin out of his sight.

Weather-wise, it was another perfect day just like the day before. I wondered what Mom would have planned had the weather been cold and rainy. Knowing her imagination, there would have been reckless treasure hunts, questionable indoor pool activities and bar games like beer pong.

As we rode, I thought about the conversation I had had with Mom and Chas the day before. Chas was serious about me opening for him, and I thought I could do it. Three months before it would never have occurred to me. Of course, I would want Mom, the Boys, Gus and Teddy to come, too—but only because Mom would insist.

The ride to campus seemed very short. In no time, I could see the tall brick wall that surrounded the campus. It seemed as long as the Great Wall and equally as menacing to intruders.

We approached the massive iron gates with the school's crest proudly mounted. The gates had been opened, as they were each morning, and I could see the straight road with the line of trees running along each side and the chapel in the distance.

We rode through the gates and under the allée of oak trees. We passed my dorm on the hill on the right and the small lake on the left with the library above it. Sunlight flickered through the leaves but as we approached the end I could see blue sky and the treeless green lawn that surrounded the chapel.

My classmates were all on their way to chapel until they heard us coming and stopped in their tracks. Much to the bishop's dismay, I'm sure, those who had already entered came rushing out to catch one last glimpse of Tess. I saw Deidre and Drew and knew they would wait for me to enter even though we couldn't sit together.

We parked the bikes on the road away from the chapel. We all got off and took off our helmets and gloves. After I hugged Trey, Teddy, and Gus, they got back on their bikes. Mom kissed my forehead and we hugged like we were never going to see each other again. She stood and watched as I picked up my helmet and gloves and began running toward the chapel.

I got halfway there but then dropped my helmet and gloves and turned around. We ran to each other and held on like we were bracing for a hurricane. By this time, we were both sobbing, and it was hard for the men to watch. Teddy bowed his head and shook it from side to side. Gus probably longed to hold both of us in his arms. And I think Trey wanted to abscond with me.

Finally, Mom held me away from her, tears still streaming down her face.

"Love you," she said.

"Love you more," I said.

She shook her head. "Not possible."

When I reached the chapel door, I turned back and waved to my family.

55
Chapel

eidre, Drew and I hugged and then went quickly to our assigned seats. I had never had as many greetings as I did between the time I entered the chapel and the time I sat down.

Tate and Judith managed to say, "Great to see you! Hope you had a nice weekend." I found the obsequious fawning a little pathetic. I was, after all, the same person I'd been two days before. Fortunately, most of the people here knew that.

As Bishop Gates blathered on and on, thoughts were racing through my head. What was I doing here? Being homeschooled, I had already completed many of the requirements necessary for college. I could earn the rest a lot faster with my tutors. Here, it was all about finishing and trying to show that I was "well rounded" in order to get into a "good" college. But did I even want to go to college?

In my adolescent angst and petulance, I thought Mom should never have had a child. I thought she had smothered, stifled, and suffocated me. What I now realized was that she had done the best she knew how to love and protect me. She never had a role model in her formative years, so she had to make it up as she went along.

I had been desperately searching for affirmation. I wanted to grow to be my own person, but I realized she was the voice in my head: Be patient, be kind, work hard. Be a person of good character even when no one is watching.

And then I had an epiphany. I *didn't* want to live in her shadow. I wanted to live in her *light.*

I wanted to appreciate everything I had been given and become a person she would be proud of. I loved her with all my heart and wouldn't trade places with anyone in the world.

My "new normal" had had a rocky start but I had done it. I had made friends and, unfortunately, enemies as well. I had learned that although everyone experiences pain, life does grow around wounds...in small increments over time.

I was growing from my so-called life here at school and starting to have an adult-to-adult relationship with Mom. I knew that it was a work in progress but she had seen an improvement in my attitude because of this separation and I wanted it to continue.

I think Mom and Gus were enjoying their time together and although I knew they missed me, they were moving on. They deserved a chance to live and to love. I had to move on, too.

After a final prayer, we were dismissed. Deidre, Drew and I all met in the central aisle of the chapel and walked out together. We looped arms, me in the middle, as we headed for the carved wooden doors.

Drew couldn't wait to speak. "You've got to tell us all about your weekend! And we have some real "gos" to tell you! You wouldn't believe—"

Deidre interrupted him. "Never mind about the gossip. Fall Fling is this weekend and the surprise school that we're connecting with is Channing! They have the best-looking guys!"

The three of us giggled our way out the doors and as we turned the corner, I saw it. *Mom's Harley was on the edge of the lawn.*

The strap of the Strad violin case had been hooked onto the handlebars—two beautifully crafted pieces of art together as one masterpiece.

I stared in disbelief. Was this one last-ditch effort to get me to come back? Or was Mom so distraught that she felt she couldn't ride? Why did they leave the violin? I was so confused.

Miss Meyers stood amongst all of the students, looking at it. "Oh, my, we must move that somewhere."

"Yes, ma'am," I said, and started across the lawn.

When I reached the bike, I saw the key in the ignition. I put on my helmet and gloves and then strapped the violin case on my back.

I held the brake as I got on, and looked back for a moment at Deidre and Drew. I nodded to them, pulled down my face shield, and started the bike.

As I rode, I could feel the bike warm up to me as I warmed up to it. The wind whipped around me as I began to move faster and faster. I could feel the rumble throughout my whole body.

It was the same road I'd entered the campus on thirty minutes earlier, but it looked and felt different as the rider.

I looked straight ahead. Everything was a blur on either side of the road—the lake, the library, my dorm. My life.

I was at full throttle approaching the gates when I...

About the Author

MARIE WOOLF has one husband, one daughter, one cat (her muse), and one dog, because if you have the best, one is enough.

She and her husband Brian live in Greenville, South Carolina.